How ~~Not~~
To Be a
~~ROCKSTAR'S~~
Girlfriend

CASH & THE SINNERS

D. E. Haggerty

Also by D.E. Haggerty

For my dad. The original crotchety old man.

Chapter 1

Mercy – an out of work mechanic who's about to find out not everyone loves a combustion engine

MERCY

"You have got to be kidding me," I grumble at the sound of the police siren.

I check my speedometer. I'm going the speed limit. Fine. I'm going five over. But five over is pretty much the speed limit.

Maybe the police officer isn't flashing his lights at me? But there's no one else on this country road in the middle of nowhere Colorado. Crap on an oily cracker.

I pull over and switch off the engine. The engine gives a death rattle and the car jerks before it stops. I feel my cheeks heat with embarrassment. Stupid ugly car.

I roll down the window and watch as the police officer saunters toward me. Ay caramba! If all the men in Winter Falls are as sexy as him, I have landed myself in hottie heaven.

Too bad I've sworn off men. But I can look. And drool.

"Hello, officer," I greet as he stops at my window. "I don't think I was speeding."

I bite my bottom lip and try my best to appear innocent. Oh wait. I am innocent. Nearly forgot since it's a rare occurrence.

"You were going three over."

Is he seriously going to ticket me for going three over? What a fussy pants.

"But I didn't pull you over for speeding."

Phew. Such a relief since my checking account currently has a grand total of sixty-eight dollars in it.

"But you are breaking the town ordinance."

"Town ordinance?" What does a town ordinance have to do with me?

He slaps the roof of the car and I cringe. A week ago I was driving a blue Shelby GT350 with a white racing stripe down the middle. I loved my Shelby girl. I miss her more than the asshole who stole her from me.

Zeke. What a scumbag. Good luck keeping the business afloat without your free woman power.

"Cars with combustion engines are not allowed in Winter Falls."

I gasp. "Not at all?"

"Nope."

"But what other cars are there?" When he opens his mouth to speak, I hold up a hand to stop him.

"No, you can't tell me an electric engine in a car is the same. It's not. I'll admit the acceleration of a car with an electric engine is pretty rad but otherwise? No. It's not a car. The engine doesn't growl. There's no rumble of power beneath you when you drive. And what's the fun in a car you don't need to manually shift?"

He chuckles. "Enjoy your engines, do you?"

I smile. "I do. I'm a mechanic." I hold out my hand. "Mercy Keller."

"Peace Sky."

"Peace? You're a police officer and you're name is Peace?" I slap my hand over my mouth. "Sorry, officer. I didn't mean to make fun of your name."

"You're fine." He clears his throat. "But I can't allow you to operate this vehicle within the limits of Winter Falls."

"But how am I supposed to get to my destination?"

"You can park at the *Inn on Main.* I assume you're staying there."

Stay at some snooty sounding inn? I wish. I've been sleeping in my car for the past two days.

"Um, no. I'm here to visit my uncle Mercury."

His eyebrows practically fly off his head. "Old Man Mercury is your uncle?"

I get his skepticism. I can hardly believe it myself. Mom always claimed we didn't have any family while I was growing up. But suddenly last week she up and tells me I need to go to Winter Falls and put my uncle in a nursing home and sell his house.

I'm not sure about putting an uncle I've never met before in a nursing home, but I'm out of options of where to live. I'm certainly not living with Mom. Never again.

Peace scratches his beard. "I'll escort you to his house, but once you're there, you can't be driving this vehicle around Winter Falls."

I throw up my hands. Fine by me. I don't want to be driving this heap of crap anyway.

I wait until he's back in his police vehicle where he can't hear my car to switch it on. *Come on, Betsie. Come on. You can do it. A few more miles. You got this.*

When I bought Betsie, I did the best I could to make her roadworthy. But there's not a lot I could do with an engine that hasn't been maintained in twenty years and no cash. I'm planning to sell her off for parts once I make it to my uncle's house.

My uncle. Those words feel foreign to me. A frisson of excitement courses through me. I have family. I wonder what he's like.

I wait until the police car pulls in front of me and follow it. We reach the downtown of Winter Falls, and I scan the area.

Main Street is lined with Mom and Pop stores. No big box stores here. The names of the businesses – *Bake Me Happy, Eden's Garden, Bertie's Studio, Naked Falls Brewing* – pique my curiosity. What kind of place is Winter Falls?

We turn off Main Street at the square where there's an adorable little park and gazebo. We continue for a few blocks until there are no longer any houses. My excitement dims. Where is hottie police officer taking me?

Please, please, please, do not let this be the start of a horror movie. My life has been enough of a horror lately. Although, considering my propensity for making bad choices, it would be just my luck to end up in a town where they kill off anyone who dares to drive a combustion engine.

The police car turns into a driveway, and I breathe a sigh of relief. Maybe I'm not being murdered today after all. But then I notice the house.

To say it's seen better days is an understatement. It reminds me of the ghost house on my street when I was growing up. The grass is overgrown, the paint is chipped and peeling, and the windows are all covered in sheets instead of curtains.

I stop behind the police car and Betsie sputters before smoke plumes from the engine and she dies. I don't think I'm going to be able to resuscitate her. At least I made it to my destination. Such as it is.

I climb out of the car as an elderly man steps onto the porch. He leans heavily on his cane as he hobbles forward.

"What are you doing here, Peace? Don't tell me those dang busybodies sent you out here to check on me? I'm fine."

"I brought you a present." Peace points to me. "Your niece."

I wave at him. "Hi! You must be Mercury."

"Mercy." He nods. "Took you long enough to get here."

Wait. Was he expecting me? Before I can ask him, he whirls around and marches back inside the house. Um… What do I do now?

"Do you need help with your luggage?" Peace asks.

I wave him away. I don't need anyone to witness this awkward meeting. "I got it."

I wait until he's gone before approaching the house. My stuff in the car can wait until I figure out what's happening here. Did Mom phone and tell him I was coming? I snort. Mom actually be considerate? I'm not holding my breath.

I knock on the screen door. "Uncle Mercury?"

"What are you waiting for? A personal invitation?"

Well, yeah, I was. But not anymore.

I enter the house and wait a few moments for my eyes to adjust to the darkness inside. I study the place as I walk toward the living area where Mercury is sitting on a rocking chair.

"Let me guess," he begins and I startle. His booming voice is going to take some time to get used to. "Your mother never told you I existed."

I sit on the edge of the sofa. "I didn't know I had any family. She always said there was no one else."

He grunts. "Your mom isn't solely to blame. The rift began with your grandmother."

I lean closer. I don't know anything about my grandmother. Mom refuses to speak about her family.

"Lyra was Adhara's sister."

I wait but he doesn't explain further. "Who's Lyra and who's Adhara? And why do they have such weird names?"

He scowls at me. "Ain't nothing wrong with the name Adhara."

"Sorry," I mumble. I tend to blurt out whatever comes to my mind without thinking. Mom always said this tendency is going to get me into trouble one day. I hope today is not that day.

"Adhara was my wife."

I'm catching on now. "And Lyra was my grandmother?"

He nods. "Lyra didn't approve of Adhara's lifestyle."

"Lifestyle? What did she do? Run away and join a hippie commune?"

Mercury glares at me. "You have a problem with hippies, girl?"

I bite my lip as I contemplate my answer. The names of the businesses in town flash in my mind. I'm starting to connect the dots.

"Is Winter Falls a hippie commune? I didn't think those existed anymore."

"Started out as one. Now all anyone cares about is pagan festivals."

Pagan festivals? Where in the hell did I end up?

Mercury clears his throat. "Lyra cut Adhara out of her life."

"Which is why I never heard of you before," I finish. "Although, I never met my grandmother either."

He purses his lips. "You never met your grandmother?"

"Mom got pregnant with me when she was young and her mom kicked her out. Mom never talks about my grandmother. She didn't tell me about your existence until last week."

"And now you're here to put me in a goddamn old fogy's home."

He's on to me. The jig is up.

Chapter 2

Gibson — a rockstar who's about to learn a smile and a wink can't get him everything he wants

GIBSON

"Here you are." The waitress, Cheyenne according to her name tag, sets the burger in front of me. "If you won't be needing anything else?"

She has a certain gleam in her eye. It says I can drag her into the nearest closet and she'll let me have my wicked way with her. The joys of being a rockstar never get old.

"I'll be needing your number." I waggle my eyebrows at her. She tears off a piece of paper from her order pad and hands it to me. I smirk. She had her number ready for me.

"Thanks." I wink.

"We'll have another round of beers," Cash says, and Cheyenne startles.

Her eyes widen on Cash. I hold back my sigh. It's always this way. I can get a woman to drop her panties for me but they still stare at Cash as if he's a god because he's the lead singer of our band, *Cash & the Sinners.*

I should have never agreed to the name. The Sinners would have been fine. Why did we need to add the whole 'Cash &'-part?

"I love your new song," Cheyenne breathes out.

Cash smirks as he throws his arm around Indigo. "I wrote it for her."

Cheyenne sighs, and I roll my eyes. Our manager tried to talk Cash out of telling the world about his love for Indigo. He claimed it would 'hurt his image'. I wish. Instead, women crush on Cash even more. Apparently, a bad boy who settles down is catnip to women. Good thing I am never settling down.

"It's beyond romantic how all of the band members are falling in love."

I wish Cheyenne was exaggerating or this was some rumor the paparazzi thought up. Unfortunately, it's true. My bandmates are falling faster than female fans when I take my shirt off.

First Cash got back together with his high school sweetheart, Indigo. After which, Dylan – the lead guitarist – fell for Virginia, a shy librarian. And now, Fender – the grumpy bass player who claimed he'd never fall for a woman again – is smitten with Leia.

Only Jett and I are left over. I catch the drummer's eyes and feign gagging. He laughs. The two of us are of the same mind. No girlfriends. No attachments. And definitely none of this love bullshit.

"When are you leaving?" I ask Jett once the waitress saunters away.

He shrugs. "The surfing competition isn't for a few weeks yet."

Jett's an adrenaline junkie. He's never met an adventure he didn't want to try. I think it's hilarious. The rest of the band thinks otherwise. So, he missed the sound check in Vegas because he was ziplining across the grand canyon. Big deal.

"You going to scream like a baby when you get in the water again?"

He glares at me. "I did not scream like a baby when I got in the water. I yelled because there was a shark in the water. It bit one of the surfers."

"And you passed out from the sight of blood."

"I do not pass out at the sight of blood."

Cash grunts. "If he passed out at the sight of blood, he never would have been able to message us when he got a compound fracture while he was hiking El Caminito del Rey in Spain."

Dylan frowns. "We had to delay the concert in Lisbon for over a week."

Jett grunts. "You can't bitch when I played with a broken leg."

"Dude," I begin. "It's a good thing we fly in a private plane. Getting through security with all the metal you have in your body would be a trial."

"Why is everyone picking on me?" Jett asks. "I'm not the one who asked for the waitress' number in front of everyone."

Fender rolls his eyes. "You already had it."

"Whoa. You got the waitress' number before me?" I ask Jett.

"Her name is Cheyenne."

I rear back. "You remember their names now?"

"I always remember their names."

Cash growls. "Can you stop showing off your man whore tendencies in front of my woman?"

Indigo elbows him. "What are you? A caveman? You gonna drag me out of here by my hair next?"

His eyes heat. "If you want me to pull your hair, all you have to do is ask."

I lean forward. "Now, we're talking. Do you usually engage in hair play? How about spanking with a hairbrush?"

Virginia groans and covers her face. "I don't want to know."

Dylan slaps my shoulder. "Don't embarrass Ginny."

"Boring." I down my beer.

My bandmates frown at me. I know they think I'm drinking too much, but I have it under control. I'm not an alcoholic. And I'm not discussing my drinking.

I stand. "Who's ready to hit up *Electric Vibes*?"

I throw some cash on the table and aim for the door. *Electric Vibes* is a hippy bar in Winter Falls. It's the *only* bar in Winter Falls. Lucky for me, it's a cool place to hang out. It's two doors down from the brewery, *Naked Falls Brewing,* where the band had dinner.

Everything's close in Winter Falls. You can walk from one end of the town to the other in less than thirty minutes. What is a world-famous band doing here? I have no idea. We originally came to record our album at *Bertie's Recording Studio* and never left.

I'm ready to hit the road to promote our new album but the lovebirds don't want to go anywhere. In fact, we aren't doing our typical world tour. We're doing mini-tours for a year.

I'm bored and ready to do something else but I don't know what. We've been recording or touring constantly for ten years now. I don't know what to do with myself when I'm not occupied with the band. If I did, I'd be out of Winter Falls in a flash.

When we arrive at the bar, there's a woman squaring off with Old Man Mercury at the door. Old Man Mercury is one of the original founders of Winter Falls. He puts Fender's grumpiness to shame.

"I don't care, Uncle Mercury," the woman screeches as she stands in front of the bar to block Mercury from entering.

"Get out of my way, Mercy," he grumbles at her.

"No. You shouldn't be drinking."

I bristle. I hate it when someone tells me not to drink. I imagine Mercury feels the same way.

"I'll drink if I damn well want to."

"The doctor said—"

"I don't give a shit what the doctor said."

I stroll up to them. "If the man wants a drink, let him drink."

The woman whirls on me. I freeze when those dark brown eyes the color of a nice stout beer glare at me. My gaze roams over the rest of her. Her hair is auburn, the color of amber ale, and her lips are dark red. The woman's a knockout.

I want her in my bed. I want those lips swollen from my kisses, my hands fisting those auburn strands, and her dark brown eyes overcome with passion. My cock twitches. He's on board.

Thank fuck. He's been a bit bored of the women I've brought to bed lately. But this woman – Mercy I believe her name is – intrigues him as she does me.

"I don't recall asking for your opinion," she growls at me. "In fact, I don't know who you are."

"Gibson Lewis." I bow. "At your service."

"Whatever." She turns away to face Old Man Mercury again. "Mercury, you said—"

Hold on. Is she seriously ignoring me? Me, the rockstar?

Mercury wags a finger at her. "No, I didn't. You assumed."

I force my way in front of Mercy. "Excuse me. Do you not know who I am?"

She plants her hands on her hips. "Can you not see I'm busy?"

"She's awesome," Indigo declares behind me. "She's going to be my next bestie."

I ignore Indigo and make another attempt to capture Mercy's attention. "But—"

Jett snags my wrist and drags me away from her. "Try to accept your defeat with some grace."

I can't keep my eyes off this woman. "She didn't know who I was," I mutter.

"Not everyone knows who we are."

In my experience, they do. Usually, we're surrounded by fans wherever we go. Winter Falls is the one place where we can be ourselves. The press has tried to intrude several times but the inhabitants of this quirky town have managed to drive them away each time.

Fender clears his throat. "Shall we go inside?"

"I'm with Fender," Dylan says as he clasps Virginia's hand.

Cash leads Indigo to the bar. At the door, Indigo stops to wave at Mercy. "See you later."

I step toward Mercy. Jett tries to block me. "Let it go."

I can't let it go. I'm intrigued by this beauty who is pretending not to know who I am. Yes, pretending. There's no way she doesn't know who I am. She's playing hard to get. Fine. I'll chase her.

I nudge Jett out of the way and stalk to Mercy. "Mercy."

She whirls around. "You again?"

"Have you heard of the band *Cash & the Sinners?*"

"Cash and the who?"

She's laying it on thick now.

"You know. *Cash & the Sinners.* World famous rock band."

She rolls her eyes. "I don't listen to rock. I'm a country girl."

My brow wrinkles. A country girl? My gaze roves over her. The black t-shirt she's wearing is loose but the neckline is low enough for me to catch a glimpse of her cleavage. I want more than a glimpse.

Her t-shirt's tucked into a pair of worn jeans. The material hugs her hips and have holes in her knees. I bet those legs would feel fabulous wrapped around my hips as I plunge into her. On her feet are a pair of cowboy boots.

"I don't mind country girls," I finally say once I'm done checking her out.

"But I mind rockers."

I rear back. "Excuse me?"

I've never met a woman who didn't jump at the chance to be with a rocker before. I didn't think they existed.

The door shuts behind her and she peers over her shoulder. "Damn. Mercury got away."

She rushes after him without a second glance at me. Huh. She wasn't kidding about not knowing who I am.

Challenge accepted.

Chapter 3

Mercury – an old man who is the reason the term grumpy old man was invented

MERCY

"What in tarnation are you doing?"

I jump at Mercury's booming voice and whirl around.

"What do you think I'm doing?" I motion to the sheets on the floor.

"Looks like you're getting rid of my curtains."

"Those are not curtains. Curtains are not attached to the window with masking tape."

"It keeps the sunshine out just fine."

My nose wrinkles. "Why do you want to keep the sunshine out? I practically need a flashlight to make it to the bathroom in the middle of the day with the hallway light on as it is."

Despite accusing me of wanting to put him in a nursing home, Uncle Mercury said I could stay with him. I jumped at the chance. Staying here gives me time to figure out my next step. Not to mention my uncle should not be left to his own devices.

"Someone's prone to exaggeration," he mutters.

"Come on. It's nice with the sunshine pouring in. You can sit in your chair and feel it on your face."

"I don't want to feel sunshine on my face."

I bite my tongue before I lash out in frustration. If you look up crotchety old man in the dictionary, you'll find a picture of my great uncle. I can't do anything right. His coffee's too hot, his soup is too cold. The list goes on and on.

I'm used to my family not approving of anything I do. But Mom normally grumbles once and then checks out. Of course, she checks out with a bottle of vodka so her behavior isn't exactly good either.

"We're going to be late," Mercury announces.

"Late for what? I'm not taking you to the bar again. Trick me once, shame on you. Trick me twice, I'm an idiot."

"Hospital."

"Hospital? What's wrong? Do I need to phone an ambulance? Is there a hospital in Winter Falls? I don't think we can make it far with a golf cart."

Yes, golf cart. Since Winter Falls is anti-cars, the preferred method of transportation is a golf cart. I'm not sure how long I can stay in a town that hates cars as much as I love them.

"Calm down, woman. We'll use my car."

"You have a car? I thought no one in Winter Falls was allowed to own a car."

He grins. "I am."

I wipe the dust on my pants off on my jeans. "I'll get changed."

"No time."

"Can I at least go to the bathroom before we leave?"

"Make it quick." He doesn't wait before starting for the front door.

I rush to the bathroom. When I see myself in the mirror, I squeak. My hair is a mess of curls and there are streaks of dirt on my forehead. I braid my hair before washing my face.

I hurry out of the room to discover the front door open. I grab my phone and scurry after Mercury.

When I step on the porch, I don't see him. He better have not left without me. He shouldn't be running around by himself.

I hear the roar of an engine and excitement fills me. This isn't some golf cart. Nope. The porch vibrates with the vibrations of the V8 engine. What kind of car is Uncle Mercury hiding? And when can I drive it?

A black Dodge Charger drives around the corner. No way. No way does Uncle Mercury own this car. He's supposed to be a hippie who hates anything bad for the environment.

"You getting in or are you staring at me all day?" He shouts.

I snag my gaze from the hood to the driver's window. "I wasn't staring at you."

I run around the car and jump in the passenger's seat. "Where have you been hiding this beauty?"

He grunts. "Not hiding it. It was in the garage."

He shifts into third gear and we lurch forward. "Damn leg."

"What year is this beauty?" I ask instead of reminding him to switch from first to second before shifting into third gear.

"You know stuff about cars?"

"I'm a mechanic."

He glances over at me with his mouth gaping open. The car swerves and I grab the steering wheel. "Road."

He returns his attention to the road in front of us but can't help peeking over at me every few seconds.

"What?" I finally ask.

"I didn't expect Lyra's granddaughter to be a mechanic."

I cross my arms over my chest and glare at him. "I thought hippies were all about equality. A woman can be a mechanic just as easily as a man. In fact, my hands are smaller and can reach places asshole men can't reach."

"Asshole men?"

Crap. I slipped up. I'm not telling Mercury about my ex. The asswipe doesn't deserve a place in my mind. I shove thoughts of him and how he stole everything from me away. It's over. No use crying over spilled milk.

"Where is this hospital?"

He frowns but allows me to change the topic. "White Bridge."

"How far is White Bridge?"

"Not far."

Trust me. White Bridge feels pretty far when your great uncle is driving and keeps forgetting to press the clutch down when he shifts. I'm surprised the car didn't stall more than once.

While Mercury maneuvers the car into a parking spot, I try to come up with a way to steal his keys. I do not want to drive back to Winter Falls with him grinding the gears. My mechanic's heart is bleeding for the poor transmission.

We arrive at the reception area and I check Mercury in before taking a seat next to him to wait for the doctor.

It isn't long before a woman steps into the area and calls Mercury's name. When I stand to go with him, he glowers at me. "I don't need you to come with me."

"She can join us," the woman says. I like her already.

"I'm Mercy," I say once we enter an exam room.

"I'm Dr. Vander," she says as we shake hands.

"Is this a meet and greet or a doctor's office?" Mercury grumbles and I roll my eyes.

"Mr. Crotchety has arrived," I mumble.

Dr. Vander ducks her chin but not before I see her smile. She clears her throat. "Why don't you hop up on the exam table?"

"Hop? How do you expect me to hop? I haven't hopped anywhere in over a decade." He waves his cane at her.

I rush to him. "I'll help."

Once he's settled, I retreat to the other side of the room where I can peer outside the window and avoid seeing any of my great uncle naked. I shiver. I can handle a grumpy old man. Naked old man, on the other hand? No thanks.

"You can turn around now," Dr. Vander says as she helps Mercury to sit in a chair across from her desk a few minutes later.

I sit next to him. The doctor types on her computer while we wait. My leg bounces with impatience. What's wrong with my uncle? Should I be pushing more for him to be put in a nursing home?

"Now, Mr. Mercury," she begins.

"Mercury. No mister necessary."

"Mercury," she starts again. "as we've discussed in the past, you shouldn't be living on your own anymore."

"I'm not. My niece is living with me."

I cringe. Does he expect me to live with him forever?

"Your niece is not a health care professional who's available round-the-clock." Dr. Vander cringes. "I'm sorry. I didn't ask if you're a health care professional."

I wave away her apology. "I'm the furthest thing from a nurse. Unless you count nursing a car back to health."

She doesn't laugh at my joke. Tough crowd.

"I don't need a babysitter with me all damn day," Mercury declares.

"What if you fall?" Dr. Vander challenges. "Your knee and hip aren't getting any better."

"You're the doctor. You're supposed to make them better."

She sighs. "You don't need to be ashamed of needing a bit of help at your age."

"You're not talking about a bit of help. You want me in one of those old people's homes." Mercury glares at me. "You're as bad as her."

My face warms at the accuracy of the accusation. I should have known better than to listen to Mom. I should have known there was some catch. *Go meet your uncle and get him settled in a nursing home. It'll be easy.* Easy my ass.

"Do you remember the bronchitis you contracted last year?" Mercury grunts. "This time you might not be as lucky."

Dr. Vander stands. "Think about it."

Mercury groans as he stands. I hurry to help him but he bats me away. "I'm not a feeble old man."

"Just old then," I mutter.

We make our way out of the office and downstairs to the parking lot. I can tell by the way Mercury's leaning on his cane, he's tired. Considering his bad knee and hip, he shouldn't be driving at all, let alone a manual transmission.

"Can I drive back?"

He scowls at me.

"Come on," I beg. "Your car is a mechanic's wet dream."

"Fine," he huffs and hands me the keys. "But you're not putting me in a home."

I snatch the keys from him before he can change his mind. "Dr. Vander thinks it's a good idea."

"Dr. Vander is a quack."

"Those certificates on her walls seemed real enough."

He snorts.

"You can't stop an argument because you're losing."

"Can too."

I help him to settle in the passenger seat before rushing around to the driver's side. I inhale a deep breath to calm myself before opening the door. This isn't my car. And I probably shouldn't squeal my tires in a hospital parking lot. I hate the word should.

"What's the big deal about living in a nursing home any-way?" I ask once we're on the road and I've managed to stop myself from blowing out of town. It was a close call. My foot is still tapping the gas pedal in anticipation.

"Do you want to live in a nursing home?"

I wag a finger at him. "Nuh-huh. You can't answer a question with a question. It's against the rules."

"Who says?"

"I do."

"You're gonna run roughshod over my life, aren't you?"

I grin. "Just until you're in a nursing home."

"I'm about as likely to go in a nursing home as you are to have a boyfriend."

I gasp. "I've had boyfriends." Too many if I'm being honest with myself. Something I prefer not to do. "I can find another one."

"Sure you can."

"I can! But I don't want to."

"Don't want to or can't?"

I squeeze the steering wheel in an effort to keep my frustration under control. "Uncle Mercury, don't start with me."

"I'm not starting anything. All I'm saying is I'm not going into a nursing home until you have a boyfriend."

Crap. My little detour to Winter Falls has apparently been extended indefinitely.

Chapter 4

GIBSON

"Come on. Hurry up." Jett taps his toe as he waits for me to put my shoes on.

"What's got your panties in a twist?"

"You know I don't wear underwear."

"Yeah, but what I don't know is why someone who is constantly hurting himself wouldn't want to wear underwear for a bit of protection."

"I don't need underwear to protect my balls."

I cock an eyebrow. "I meant to protect me from seeing your dick hanging out when your pants are cut off because you broke your leg again."

"I broke my leg one time."

"Are we not counting the time you jumped off stage?"

"Whatever," he mutters since he knows I'm right.

By my count, he's broken his leg at least three times. And I'm not including all the sprains and other broken bones. The man is a daredevil who has no fear for his safety. One of these days it's going to bite him in the ass.

"Get moving. Isla's waiting for us."

For someone who claims to hate children and has declared he will never have any, Jett certainly spends a lot of time with Leia's eleven-year-old daughter.

I follow him out of our place to the house next door, which Fender shares with Leia and Isla. The door opens before we can enter and our bandmates and their girlfriends tumble outside. Dylan and Virginia are first. Fender and Leia with Isla in between them are next.

Last to exit are Cash and Indigo. Except Cash doesn't look like Cash.

"What the hell are you wearing?" I ask him.

"Language," Fender growls and points to Isla.

"Sorry. What the heck are you wearing?"

"It's a disguise," Cash answers. "Downtown will be crowded today with the Mabon festival."

"I get the baseball cap. I even get the glasses with the funny nose. What I don't get is the fat suit." His t-shirt strains against his stomach.

"It was my idea," Indigo says. "The baseball cap and glasses can't hide his sexy body. He needs to hide his sexiness or he'll be spotted by fans."

Cash wraps an arm around her and pulls her near. "You think I'm sexy."

She rolls her eyes. "Was there any doubt?"

He waggles his eyebrows. "Maybe you can—"

Fender growls. "Child present."

Isla huffs. "I'm not a child."

"She's practically twelve," Jett says and holds out his hand to her. She rushes to him. Together, they skip down the street ahead of us.

"Who else thinks it's extremely weird Jett is skipping with a child?" I ask.

Leia glares at me. "What's wrong with Isla?"

I hold up my palms and back away from her. "There's nothing wrong with Isla. The problem is Jett. He 'hates' children."

Her brow furrows. "He's been nothing but kind to my daughter."

"Thus the weirdness."

Fender reaches across Leia to smack me upside the head. "Enough," he growls.

"I thought you were going to stop being a grump since you've found love." I feign gagging on the word love. Love. Ugh. Who needs it? Not me. Love is a lie.

Leia giggles. "Fender will always be a grump."

He smiles down at her. "But I'm your grump."

"I think I'll go skip with Jett," I mutter before hurrying ahead of the three couples.

For the past decade, it's been the five of my bandmates against the world. Now, three of them are happily coupled off. At least Jett and I have a pact to never fall in love.

"What is Mabon anyway?" I ask when we arrive at Main Street.

"It's a celebration of the harvest," Indigo answers. She's a teacher at the local school and is my source for all things local.

"But how do you celebrate it?" I ask.

"I think there's a parade." Cash indicates the ropes holding people back from entering the street.

"I wonder if they'll throw candy," Isla says.

Fender picks her up and settles her on his shoulders. "Come on, cutie pie. Let's find a good spot to get some candy."

Isla giggles. "Giddy up, horsey!"

"No, not horses," someone groans from behind us. I whirl around to discover a police officer strolling toward us.

"Hey, Peace," Cash greets his half-brother.

I'm still shocked whenever I think about Cash having brothers. When we met, he was an orphan with no family. His mother died when he was in high school and he didn't have any other relatives. Or so he thought.

Turns out his biological dad had a wife and children as well as another child out of wedlock. Now Cash has six half-brothers and two women who have claimed him as his son.

My stomach sours. Knock it off. I'm not jealous. I'm happy for my bandmate.

"What's wrong with horses?" Jett asks.

Peace rubs a hand down his face. "We use horses to pull the parade floats since cars are frowned upon in Winter Falls. But Juniper is protesting the use of the horses."

I perk up. A protest could be fun. "How is she protesting?"

"A sit-in at the courthouse."

I frown. A sit-in sounds boring. Where's the loud protesting? The clash with the police? The time in jail? Maybe I can give Juniper some ideas.

"No." Peace steps in front of me.

I feign confusion. "What? No?"

He wags his finger at me. "No joining the protest."

I cross my arms over my chest. "Isn't the right to protest constitutionally protected?"

Jett comes to stand next to me. "It is. We should join them."

Dylan sighs. "No. Tweedle Dee and Tweedle Dum will not be protesting today."

I glare at him. "You can't stop me."

"What will your new lady think of your protesting?"

My brow wrinkles. "I don't have a lady."

He points behind me. I search the area until my gaze falls on Mercy. The woman who claimed she didn't know who I am. She must know who I am by now. Google doesn't lie. I think I'll go find out.

"See ya," I say and make my way to Mercy who appears to be arguing with Old Man Mercury again. I slow to listen to their argument.

"You shouldn't be walking around town," Mercy yells at Mercury.

"I'll walk around town if I damn well want to."

"The doctor said you should rest your knee and hip. You aren't the youngest anymore."

"You aren't putting me in a home."

Mercy plants her hands on her hips. "The doctor says you need round the clock care."

"The doctor says. The doctor says," Mercury grumbles.

"I can't care for you twenty-four-seven."

"Why not? It's not as if you have a boyfriend."

Mercy's nostrils flare as she glares at Mercury. "I'm not getting a boyfriend just so you'll agree to live in a nursing home."

Hold on? Is this my opportunity? Does she need a boyfriend? I don't do the boyfriend/girlfriend thing but I can fake it. I do enjoy any chance to pull one over on my bandmates.

"Hey, Mercy," I holler.

She glances my way and those dark brown eyes I want to watch light up with passion fill with confusion.

"Do I know you?"

"We met at the bar."

She frowns and my gaze snags on those dark red lips. Those full lips will look sexy as fuck stretched around my cock. My pants tighten in response to the vision.

"I don't remember you."

I chuckle. She must be joking.

"I'm serious."

"You were arguing with Mercury then, too."

She sighs. "You aren't exactly narrowing things down."

"He wanted a drink. You were barring him from entry to the bar."

"Sounds familiar," she mutters. "This guy doesn't listen."

She glances toward Mercury but he's gone.

"Did you let him sneak off?"

I motion to where he's sitting next to Clove. "He's there."

Her shoulders fall in relief. "Who knew my uncle would be such a pain in my ass?"

"Old Man Mercury is your uncle?"

"So I'm told."

"Since your uncle's safe, why don't you and I watch the parade together?" I waggle my eyebrows to make it clear I'm not referring to watching the actual parade.

"I don't even know you. Why would I go anywhere with you?"

"I'm Gibson Lewis, remember? I told you who I was when we met. Didn't you google me?"

She rears back. "Google you? Why the hell would I google you?"

"To figure out who I am."

"Why? Are you some famous stalker?"

"Stalker? Me?"

"You're the one who keeps insisting I google you. What do you expect me to think?"

"I didn't expect you to think I'm a stalker." I clear my throat. "Let's start over." She doesn't respond so I rush to continue. "Hi, Mercy. I'm Gibson. It's lovely to meet you."

We shake hands. "You're weird."

"I'm not used to introducing myself to people."

"Oh, are you a hermit? Is it scary for you to be amongst this many people?"

"I'm not a damn hermit," I growl.

She shrugs and I watch as her breasts jiggle with the movement. My fingers tingle to touch her, to knead her breasts, to pinch her nipples until she's crying my name.

She snaps her fingers in my face. "My eyes are up here."

"Sorry."

She snorts. "You're not sorry."

I grin. I'm not.

"This has been lovely. Not. But I need to go." She starts to leave, but I shackle her wrist to stop her.

She glares down at my hand on her, and I immediately let go and step back.

"I have a proposal for you."

She raises her eyebrows. "Why would I care?"

"It'll help get your uncle off your back."

"I'm listening."

Chapter 5

Bad boy – the last person you should make an agreement to fake date

MERCY

Gibson has a proposal for me? A proposal to help me with my uncle? I'm all ears.

Or, at least, I'm trying to be. It's hard to concentrate on the words coming out of his mouth when all I want to do is stare at him. From top to toe Gibson Lewis is catnip to me.

He has light brown hair mussed up to make it appear as if he just got out of bed. I want to run my hands through it and muss it up even more. I bet if I tug on the ends, he'll moan in pleasure.

I wonder what it would take to get those light brown eyes to darken with passion. Perhaps if I scraped my fingernails along the shadow of a beard on his chin. And those cheekbones. Holy batman. I could cut glass on those cheekbones.

I continue my perusal of his body. He's lean but I could feel his strength when he snatched my wrist.

All of the above makes for a very, very pretty package, but the icing on the top is the tattoos. He's covered in them. I do love a bad boy. And those tattoos spell bad boy in all capitals.

Good thing I'm on a break from men because Gibson Lewis has heartbreak written all over him. Heartbreak is always the end result when you fall for a player. Ask me how I know.

"Are you done?" He winks.

"Done what?"

He motions toward his body. "Realizing how sexy you think I am."

"This is a bad idea." I whirl around but he stops me again.

"Don't you want to hear my proposal?"

I scowl. "Not if it's sexual."

He sighs. "It's not." He winks. "Unfortunately."

Told you. Player.

I cross my arms over my chest and his gaze dips to my breasts. I drop my arms and plant my fists on my hips instead. "You said you can get my uncle off my back."

He clears his throat. "I do have an idea."

I motion for him to proceed.

He glances around. "Not here."

"Dude, if this is some way to get me into your bed, you're barking up the wrong tree. I don't sleep with men I don't know." Anymore. "And I don't do one-night stands." Much.

He waves toward the bakery, *Bake Me Happy,* which appears empty since everyone and their brother is standing on Main Street waiting for the parade to start.

"You're buying me the biggest latte they have and a chocolate muffin," I order as I march toward the bakery.

"Yes!" The man behind the counter shouts when we enter.

I scan the room but there's no one else here besides us. I approach with caution. I've known a lot of crazy in my life. I can handle this.

"Hello," I greet.

"Hi, Mercy," he says and I rear back.

"How do you know my name?"

He winks. "Everyone knows your name."

It's confirmed. He's crazy. "Mm hum."

He rolls his eyes. "I'm Bryan, and I'm not crazy."

Everyone who's crazy says they're not.

"I know your name because you're new to Winter Falls."

Now, I'm interested. I step closer. "Because I'm new to town? Is there a town bulletin?"

He giggles. "Yes, it's called Facebook."

"Hey." Gibson joins me at the counter. "I'm on Facebook but I didn't read anything about Mercy arriving in Winter Falls.

"Duh. Rockstars don't check their own social media."

"Rockstar?" My nose wrinkles. "Who's a rockstar?"

Bryan points to Gibson. "He is."

"You are?"

Gibson grins. "I'm the rhythm guitarist for *Cash & the Sinners*."

"I'm guessing by the way you said the name you think I should know the band *Cash & the Sinners*."

Bryan laughs. "But you don't. This is precious. Absolutely precious. We need to re-do the odds calculations."

"The odds calculations?" What in the world is going on here?

"Never you mind," he sings.

I shove my questions and concerns about this small town away. Winter Falls can be as kooky as it wants. I'm not here to stay. I'm here to move my uncle into a nursing home and sell his house, and then I'll skedaddle. Too bad my uncle cottoned onto my plan within minutes of my arrival.

"Can I get the biggest caramel mocha latte you have and whatever chocolate treat you recommend? The 'rock star' is buying."

Bryan motions to the display case. "Pick out what you want. We don't have much left since the tourists nearly picked us clean."

I study the treats and my mouth waters. There are chocolate chip cookies, oatmeal raisin muffins, slices of carrot cake, and raspberry brownies. I want it all.

"She'll have one of each," Gibson orders from behind me.

I start to protest but why bother? It's not as if I'll get a chance to come into town often – dealing with Uncle Mercury is a full-time job – and these goodies appear scrumptious.

Gibson places a hand on my lower back and tingles erupt where he's touching me. I don't revel in those tingles. Nope. I'm on a break from men. Especially rockstars who think they're god's gift to women. Tingles be damned.

I settle in a chair at the table furthest away from Bryan. I've known the man for a grand total of five minutes but he has eavesdropper written all over him. As someone who's been dubbed nosy for most of her life, I can spot a fellow busybody a mile away.

I wait until Bryan places our coffees and treats on the table before speaking.

"Well?"

Gibson merely stares at me.

"What's your proposal?" I ask and pick up my coffee for a sip.

"We date."

I sputter and my coffee flies out of my mouth straight at Gibson's face. He grabs a napkin to wipe the liquid away.

"Your fault, dude. You should have waited until I wasn't drinking to reveal your idiotic idea. In case this is unclear." I lean forward to hiss at him. "I'm not dating you."

Hurt flashes in his light brown eyes but I ignore it. No way is a rockstar truly upset I turned him down. His pride might be. But the man himself? Nope.

"I don't want to date you either."

"If you don't want to date me, why did you say you want to date? Is the rock music rotting your brain? You should listen to country. It's way better."

He rolls his eyes. "I don't want to listen to someone cry about losing their man or their job and being broke."

Guess he doesn't want to hear about my life then since he literally described my recent past. Lost my man? Check. Lost my job? Check. Broke? Check. Add in the part about the man stealing the woman's business and it's a perfect match.

"Country music is about real people with real feelings not banging on the drums."

"I don't play the drums. I play the guitar."

"Whatever." I throw up my hands. "Us dating is obviously not going to work."

"Which is why we won't be dating." He leans close to whisper, "We'll pretend to date."

"I don't want…" I trail off when I realize he said pretend. I can pretend. I can pretend until the cows come home and are all milked.

Wait a minute. He's a rockstar. Allegedly. Why would he want to fake date little old me? What's he getting out of this?

"Why?" I ask.

"Why what?"

I huff. "Why do you want to fake date me?"

"I have my reasons. Does it matter? This will help you with your uncle. Don't you want to help your uncle?"

What I want is a man to be honest with me for a change.

"Tell me what your angle is or I'm out the door." I glance down at the goodies on the table. "As soon as Bryan boxes all these up."

He purses his lips as he thinks about it. I grab the brownie and shove it in my face while he figures out a way to lie to me. You know he's going to lie. No way some rockstar will tell me the truth.

I'm starting on the cheesecake when he finally speaks.

"I want my bandmates off my back."

"Have they been pressuring you to get a girlfriend?"

"Not exactly."

I wave my fork at him. "You think some more about whether you can be honest with me while I finish this up."

He blows out a breath. "Fine. They think I drink too much."

I freeze with the fork poised at my mouth. He's a drinker? This isn't going to work. I've had enough of dealing with people who prefer a bottle over me.

"I'm not an alcoholic," he grumbles.

"And I've never heard those words before."

"I'm serious."

I set my fork down and wipe my mouth with the napkin as I contemplate this. I have an idea. It'll probably piss him off, but better he loses his shit now before we begin this charade.

"If we do this." He grins but I hold up a hand. "I said *if*." He motions for me to proceed. "There will be ground rules."

"What rules?"

"No drinking and no other women."

"No drinking at all?"

I shrug. "If you can't handle it, it's fine. I won't tell anyone about this conversation." I make as if to stand. He places a hand on mine to stop me.

"Fine. But I have rules, too."

"Go ahead."

"You'll go to all social activities with the band."

"I have my uncle to care for. I can't be at your beck and call."

"You'll come to as many social activities as possible. You'll pretend to be besotted with me. And you won't use your uncle as an excuse to hide away."

Damn him. He's covered every angle. I rack my brain, but I can't think of any other way to get my uncle to agree to move into a nursing home.

I hold out my hand. "Deal."

"Deal." We shake, and I ignore the tingles erupting on my skin from contact with his. This is fake. It isn't real. It'll never be real. I don't date bad boys anymore.

"Now finish your goodies and I'll tell you all about the band."

I make a face. "I don't listen to rock music."

"If you were my real girlfriend, you'd know about the band."

He has a point. "Go ahead, fake man of mine. Tell me all about your life. I'm dying to hear it all."

Unfortunately, I'm not lying. At least, not completely. I am curious about this man sitting in front of me. I do love me a bad boy.

No. No more bad boys.

No more men.

I'm on a break from them.

Now to get my hormones on board.

Chapter 6

Couple – a word that causes nervous tremors in a certain rockstar

GIBSON

I scan Leia's backyard where the party is in full swing. We're celebrating her forgiving Fender for being an idiot and the two of them becoming a couple.

Couple. The last thing I want to be is in a couple. Except I'm supposed to be pretending to be in one. Where is my country girl anyway? I'm anxious to see her.

I pull out my phone and message her.

Come to the party.

When she doesn't respond, I text again.

Please.

When she still doesn't respond, I bring out the big guns.

You promised.

I'm getting annoyed – she did promise to attend social events with me as my girlfriend – when she messages me back.

Fine.

Even her texts are full of sass. Usually, I don't care what a woman has to say. There's no need for talk in the bedroom. With Mercy, it's different. She's different.

> **I'm here.**

At Mercy's message she's arrived, I hurry to intercept her. As I round the house, Mercy steps out of a classic Dodge Charger. The car is black and in pristine condition. I whistle.

"Are you whistling at me or the car?"

I wink. "Can't it be for both?"

She rolls her eyes.

I'm not lying. The car is sexy. But so is she. She's wearing cut-off jeans showing off miles of tanned legs with a pair of cowboy boots.

I force my gaze off those legs I want wrapped around my waist and notice her black t-shirt says *My neighbors listen to country music whether they like it or not.* I smile. My sassy girl chose this t-shirt to piss me off but I'm not falling into her trap. She can rave about her choice in music all she wants. Rock will always be better.

She slams the car door shut. "Let's do this."

"You can at least pretend to be excited."

"Excited about what?"

"Me. I am a catch, you know." I waggle my eyebrows.

She huffs. She's not excited today, but I'll change her mind. Eventually.

I hold out my hand. She scowls at me and I wiggle my fingers. "Girlfriends hold their boyfriend's hand."

I don't have any personal experience with the matter but I've watched three of my bandmates fall in love over the past year. Cash, Dylan, and Fender can't keep their hands off their women.

"Fine," she mutters.

When our hands meet, a spark of electricity runs from her hand to mine and through my body heating me from within. My cock twitches. He's fully onboard with this development.

I ignore it. I knew I was attracted to Mercy when we made this fake relationship deal. I also knew I wasn't going to act on it. I don't do relationships and Mercy has relationship written all over her.

"Whoa!" Jett skids to a stop in front of us. "Who's this? And why are you holding her hand?"

I push him. "Why do you think I'm holding her hand?"

"You're afraid she'll run away."

Mercy giggles.

"Hi!" Jett greets her with a smirk. "I'm Jett. Dump him and I'll show you a night to remember."

I growl at him. "No. Leave her alone. She's mine."

Mercy nods in agreement, and Jett's eyes widen. "Does this mean I won?"

Fuck. I forgot all about the stupid bet. Mercy's going to run away faster than the V8 engine in the Dodge Charger can carry her when she learns about it.

"Won what?" She asks.

"Nothing," I insist.

She ignores me. "Tell me more, Jett."

Jett opens his mouth to answer, but I don't let him. I tackle him and we fall to the ground as we wrestle with each other.

Indigo rushes over to Mercy. "What are they arguing about?"

I continue to fight with Jett. I trust Indigo to not tell Mercy about the bet. She's too interested in me finding love, which is one of the reasons I decided to start this whole charade in the first place.

"Do I know you?" Mercy asks.

"Indigo. We met outside the bar when you were fighting with your uncle."

Virginia and Leia join the group of women. "This is Virginia and Leia. Virginia is with Dylan and Leia is with Fender."

Leia points to us wrestling on the ground. "What are they doing now?"

"Fighting over some bet Jett claims he won," Mercy answers. "Don't ask me what the bet's about." She sounds as if she doesn't care. My fake girlfriend should care I'm fighting.

"Did you come here with Gibson?" Leia asks and I strain to hear Mercy's answer.

"Yeah. We're dating."

Relief courses through me. She's sticking to our story. While I'm off guard, Jett uses the opportunity to throw a left hook at me. I manage to block him before he can pummel my face. I lose track of the conversation as I grapple with Jett.

The next thing I hear is Leia saying, "Gibson and Jett have an ongoing bet on who can sleep with the most women."

Shit. I am in deep trouble here. I shove Jett away and jump to my feet. "Not anymore. I'm a one-woman man now."

Jett snorts behind me. "I'll believe it when I see it."

I stand next to Mercy and throw my arm around her shoulders. Her body is stiff so I massage her shoulder until she relaxes. There's my girl.

"It's true. Mercy is the only woman for me."

"Cash, Dylan, Fender!" Jett hollers for our other bandmates, and they hurry to us.

"What's going on? What's wrong?" Dylan asks as he stands in front of Virginia as if to protect her. The man goes to extreme lengths when it comes to protecting his woman.

Jett glares at us. "Gibson is dating a woman."

"Mercy, these are my bandmates Cash, Dylan, and Fender," I introduce her and she waves in greeting at them. "Guys, this is Mercy. We're dating."

"Dating?" Dylan's mouth gapes open. "Do you know what dating means?"

I flip him off. "Asshole."

"Does she know who you are?" Cash asks.

Mercy rolls her eyes. "He's a rockstar. He has tons of fans. Women throw their panties at him. Yadda. Yadda. Yadda. Rock isn't my genre." She waves toward her t-shirt.

Indigo giggles. "I hadn't noticed your t-shirt. Anyone who wears *that* t-shirt to a party with a rock band is going to be my new best friend."

"Leave the girl alone," Virginia says. "She's ready to run as it is."

I glance down at Mercy. Is she ready to run? Her gaze darts around the backyard as if searching for an escape hatch. Yep. She's getting ready to bolt. I tighten my hold on her.

"Indigo's harmless," I tell her.

"Unless she sics her cat on you." Cash does an exaggerated shiver.

Indigo elbows him. "Katy Purry wouldn't hurt a fly."

"Because she prefers to kill birds and frogs and squirrels," Cash claims.

"I have got to meet this cat," Mercy mutters.

Indigo beams at Mercy. "We'll have a girls' night out at my place."

"I don't know about this," I start.

Will Mercy be able to keep this cover of us dating when she's being interrogated by Indigo, Virginia, and Leia? Virginia's fine. She's shy and won't pressure Mercy. Indigo and Leia, on the other hand? Neither one of them will hesitate to barrage Mercy with questions.

Mercy pats my stomach. "It'll be fine."

"Don't you need to care for your uncle Mercury in the evenings?"

She shrugs. "He goes to bed super early."

"Your uncle?" Indigo asks. "Old Man Mercury is your uncle?"

"Old Man?" Mercy snorts. "It fits. I call him Mr. Crotchety."

Indigo gasps. "To his face?"

"What's he going to do? Hit me with his cane? He can't move very fast."

"You know his house is haunted?" Indigo grabs Mercy and tries to pull her away. I stop her. Mercy didn't agree to be friends with my bandmates' girlfriends when she agreed to fake date me.

I grasp Mercy's hand and lead her to the side of the house away from my nosy bandmates. "Are you okay?"

Her brow wrinkles. "Why wouldn't I be?"

"Indigo is pretty pushy."

"Trust me. I know what pushy is and she ain't it."

"You don't have to stay if you don't want to."

"I can stay a while. I could use a break from my uncle."

I study her face for any signs of deception but she appears sincere. "Okay then." I kiss her forehead. "Off you go."

She waves as she rushes off. When I'm alone, I realize I kissed her without thinking. It was the most natural thing in the world.

Is Mercy a witch? Is she weaving a spell around me?

I need to be careful before she tricks me into falling in love with her. I can't fall in love. I've seen what 'love' does to people. No thanks. I'm opting out.

Maybe my brilliant idea to fake date her isn't as brilliant as I thought.

Chapter 7

Allergic reaction – not the same as poisoning someone. Mercy hopes.

MERCY

I pace the porch as I wait for Gibson to show. This is a disaster. I shouldn't have agreed to fake date a rockstar. My uncle is going to see through us in two seconds flat.

"Mercy!"

Speaking of the old codger.

"Yes, Uncle. What do you need?"

"I'm hungry. When is your beau getting her?"

My beau? I blow out a puff of air and stick my head in the window to talk to him. Mercury might not mind yelling but I do.

"I don't get you and your obsession with me having a boyfriend. I thought hippies were all about free love."

"Nothing wrong with free love but having a partner who loves and supports you can't be beat."

"You must have loved my aunt Adhara very much."

He coughs. "I did."

"I wish I had met her."

I don't know anything about her except that she died. I don't even know when she died. My mom didn't give me any details and Uncle Mercury isn't exactly forthcoming.

"Where is your young man?" Mercury asks. I guess he's done talking about his wife. No surprise there.

"He'll be here." I hope.

"Good. I want you settled before I move into the nursing home."

"Settled?"

He nods. "Love, marriage, babies. Settled."

"Hold on, Uncle Mercury. You can't change the deal now. You promised to go into a nursing home if I have a boyfriend. There was no talk of marriage and babies."

Is this whole fake dating agreement with Gibson for nothing? I'm certainly not marrying the man. And I'm definitely not having his babies. Is being a player hereditary? I know being an alcoholic is. I can't chance it.

"What deal?" He asks.

Is he serious? "You said—"

"Do I hear an engine?" Mercury interrupts to ask.

I glance behind me. A Hummer is pulling into the driveway. I frown when I realize the engine is electric. Some vehicles shouldn't have electric engines no matter how good it is for the environment.

Gibson exits the vehicle and waves to me before reaching inside to pull out a bunch of flowers and a bottle of wine.

He bounds up the steps toward me. "Couldn't wait to see me, country girl?"

I roll my eyes. "Let's get this over with."

"Aren't you going to kiss me hello?" He winks and I shove him away. He laughs as he rights himself.

"After you, darling." He holds the door open for me.

"Darling?"

"I was trying it on." His nose wrinkles. "No?"

"No."

We enter and I try to observe the place from his perspective. A rich rockstar who can have anything he wants. I cringe. This house is not rockstar worthy.

The floorboards creak, the windows are bare since Mercury won't let me hang curtains, the rugs are thin and non-existent in some places, and the furniture is worn. I think it's charming. Gibson probably wants to run away.

Uncle Mercury stands as we enter. I lead Gibson to him. "This is my uncle, Mercury."

Gibson smiles at him. "Nice to meet you, Mr. Mercury."

Mercury scowls. "Just Mercury. I ain't no mister."

"Mercury." Gibson offers him the bottle of wine. "This is for you."

"Can't drink. Too much medicine the voodoo doctor has me on."

"Mercy will enjoy it?" He offers the bottle to me but I refuse to accept it.

Mercury barks out a laugh. "Girl don't drink. Don't you know that?"

Gibson raises an eyebrow at me and I shrug. I'm not explaining to him how I don't drink since my mom's an alcoholic. It's none of his business. This whole boyfriend/girlfriend thing is fake.

Except my body's been humming in anticipation all day knowing Gibson would be here tonight. I ignore it. I don't have any experience ignoring my body's desires, but how hard can it be?

"These are for you, honey bun." He shoves the flowers into my hands.

I lift the bundle to my nose to smell them and immediately sneeze.

"Crap. Are you allergic to flowers?"

Mercury snorts. "Those ain't flowers. Those are weeds. Chicory weeds if I'm not mistaken."

I sneeze again and Gibson snatches the weeds from me.

"You can't buy cut flowers in Winter Falls, so I plucked these myself."

He plucked them for me? How sweet. No. Not sweet. He's playing a part. This is all an act. It's not real.

Gibson runs outside and returns with empty hands.

"What did you do with the wine?"

"Left it on the porch since no one in this room drinks."

I nod. Good. He's not drinking. I wasn't sure if I could believe him when he said he wouldn't drink as part of our deal. But I had to try. Mercury doesn't know much about my life but he knows my mom's a drinker. He would never believe Gibson's my boyfriend if he drinks.

"Shall we sit?" I indicate the table.

Gibson moves to help Mercury, but my uncle bats him away. "I can walk on my own."

Gibson scratches his chin. He appears lost and confused as he watches Mercury slowly hobble to the table.

"Sit here, young man." Mercury taps his cane on the chair next to him. "Your name is Gibson and you're in one of them rock bands?"

"Yes, sir."

"It wasn't a question."

"No, sir."

Oh crap. Mercury isn't going easy on Gibson. I need to hurry up and serve the food before Uncle Mercury figures out Gibson isn't my boyfriend.

"Do you—"

"Dinner is served!" I announce loudly to cut off my uncle's next question. "I hope you enjoy pasta."

Gibson's eyes are full of relief as he answers, "I love pasta."

"It's fettucine alfredo." I set the dish in the middle of the table and serve everyone before sitting across from Gibson.

"What about saying grace?" Mercury asks as I lift my spoon to my mouth. Gibson's spoon clatters to his plate.

I frown at Mercury. "We don't say grace."

He chortles. "But look how scared rock boy is."

Gibson's mouth is gaping open and he's frozen in his chair.

"He does appear scared."

Gibson's eyes narrow on me. "Not funny," he mutters as he picks his spoon back up and begins to eat.

I watch him as he eats. Does he like it? I'm not the best of cooks. Pasta is pretty much the only thing I can make. And even then, the sauce is from a jar. A jar I had to drive to White Bridge to buy since pre-packaged food is a big no-no in Winter Falls.

"How did you two meet?" Mercury asks.

"At the bar," I answer at the same time Gibson answers, "At the festival."

"At the bar during the festival," I amend.

"And how long have you two been dating?"

"A week," I say.

"Two weeks," Gibson says.

"Well, what is it? One week or two weeks?" Mercury demands.

I widen my eyes at Gibson and he motions for me to answer.

"We've known each other two weeks but we started dating a week ago." There. My answer sounded totally plausible. And cleared up all of the confusion. I mentally pat myself on the back. We got this.

"And what first attracted you to my Mercy?" Mercury asks and I gulp.

Crap. We don't got this. Gibson isn't 'attracted' to me. Correction. I'm sure he'd jump into bed with me if I gave him a chance. But he's not attracted to me in the traditional sense of girlfriend/boyfriend.

Gibson motions to me with his spoon. "She's beautiful."

Mercury narrows his eyes on Gibson. "She is but there's more to attraction than beauty."

"She's sas-s-s." He coughs. "Saaasy."

What the hell! He's slurring his words. He's trying to hide it but he's definitely slurring his words. Did he drink before he came here? He doesn't reek of alcohol but there are ways to hide the smell.

"Aaand smaaarth." He scratches his cheek and redness forms.

"What's wrong with you, son?" Mercury asks.

He drops his spoon. "I-I thon't snow."

I glare at him but then I realize the redness on his cheek is a rash. I gasp. "Are you allergic to pasta?"

He shakes his head. "Pees."

"You're allergic to peace?"

"Pees," he tries again.

My eyes bulge. "Peas? You're allergic to peas?"

He nods.

"I put peas in the pasta."

He scratches at his cheek. "Feel bath."

He feels bad? What do I do? I jump to my feet and run around the table. "What do you need? What can I do?"

"Anti…" He licks his lips. Oh dear. His tongue is swollen. No wonder he's slurring.

"Antihistamine?" He nods. "Will it help?" He nods again.

I rush to the bathroom. Thank god I have some antihistamines to deal with my hay fever. My hands tremble as I pick up the bottle. I drop it in the sink and it rolls around a few times before I manage to snatch it. I run back to the dining room and kneel in front of Gibson.

"Here." I shove the bottle at him. He opens it and guzzles half of the bottle in one go.

"You should probably lay down. Let me help you to the couch." I start to wrap my arm around him but he bats me away.

"Feet work."

He stumbles to the couch and falls onto it. I need to enlist some help. He shouldn't be driving. Good thing Indigo insisted on putting her number in my phone.

"Hey, bestie!" She answers on the first ring.

"Can you send someone over to Old Man Mercury's house to pick up Gibson?"

She growls. "Is he drunk?"

"He hasn't been drinking. He had an allergic reaction." Aka. I poisoned him.

"Oh." She blows out a breath. "I'll send someone over." She hangs up before I can thank her.

I throw my phone on the table and run to the couch to check on Gibson. He's passed out. I lean close to make sure he's breathing. It would be just my luck to kill a famous rockstar I'm pretending to date. I can imagine the headlines now.

Out of work mechanic poisons rockstar she was pretending to date. Was it an accident? Or is she a black widow in the making?

Nope. I force those thoughts away. He's fine. He's breathing. I push to my feet and prowl to the window. No one's here yet. I return to the couch. Gibson's still breathing. Phew. I prowl back to the window to check if anyone's on their way.

"Stop pacing. You're making me nervous," Mercury barks at me.

I wring my hands together. "I poisoned a famous rockstar."

"You didn't poison him. He has an allergy. I told you peas don't belong in pasta."

"Well, excuse me, for trying to get you to eat a few vegetables."

There's knock on the door and I rush to it.

"Mercury here?" Fender asks.

I motion to the sofa. He grunts before marching there and lifting Gibson before throwing him over his shoulder.

"Thank you," I say as I rush in front of him to open the door. "I didn't know he was allergic to peas."

"Get the door," he grumbles and I hurry to open the car door for him.

He throws Gibson in the seat and buckles him up. I frown. This appears to be a practiced routine.

"Thanks again," I say as Fender walks toward the driver's seat. He waves and gets in the car to drive away. I watch until I can't see the car's rear lights anymore.

"Welp! That's what I call a successful evening," Mercury says when I enter the house. "I'm going to bed."

Successful evening? Is he joking? What was successful about it? The part where my supposed boyfriend gave me weeds? Or maybe how he tried giving a household of teetotalers a bottle of wine? Or – and this is my favorite part – how I poisoned him?

Tonight is no one's definition of successful. I don't know how I'm going to pull off being Gibson's fake girlfriend if this is what I'm in store for.

Too bad I'm not in the market for an actual boyfriend because even with his tongue swollen and a rash on his cheek, Gibson's the sexiest man I've ever met.

Player, I remind myself. Player who enjoys drinking too much.

Chapter 8

Fake dating – apparently includes the actual act of going on a date. Who knew?

GIBSON

I groan as I roll over in bed. I'm exhausted and my head hurts. But I didn't drink last night. I was with Mercy. What happened? I remember having an allergic reaction but the rest of the night is a blank. How did I get home? I—

Whoosh! Water rains down on me.

"What the hell?" I jump out of bed.

Cash, Dylan, Fender, and Jett surround me. Jett's holding a bucket. I glare at him.

"Why did you douse me with water? I was sleeping."

"You were supposed to be at the studio rehearsing for our upcoming tour," Cash points out.

I was? What time is it? "Sorry. I forgot to set my alarm."

"Because you were drunk," Fender grumbles.

"What?" I rear back. "I wasn't drunk. I had an allergic reaction."

Dylan snorts. "An allergic reaction? Is that what we're calling it now?"

"You know I'm allergic to peas." When they continue to glare at me, I motion to Jett. "Tell them."

"I don't know what peas have to do with anything."

"Because Mercy put peas in her fettucine alfredo."

Fender grunts. "No one puts peas in fettucine alfredo."

"Mercy did." I point to my cheek. "You can probably still see the rash."

I remember scratching at my cheek before Mercy gave me some antihistamines and I promptly passed out. I probably shouldn't have chugged half the bottle but I haven't eaten peas since I first found out about my allergy.

Dylan leans close to inspect my cheek. "He does have a rash."

"Remember the time he tried a veggie burger and didn't realize it contained peas?" Jett laughs. "The rash practically covered his face."

I glare at him. "It's funny I was in agony?"

He shrugs. "You laugh whenever I break a bone."

"You jump off buildings on purpose. I don't have an allergy to peas on purpose."

"I bet Mercy felt all bad for you and kissed it better." He crosses his arms over his chest. "Or she would have if she were actually your girlfriend."

Crap. I knew this was coming. I knew my bandmates would never believe I have a girlfriend. Especially a woman they've barely met.

But I need to sell it. Really sell it. I've seen the looks they think I haven't noticed. I recognize the suspicion in their eyes. And I've dealt with Fender trying to hide my beer for months now. They're gearing up to do an intervention about my drinking.

There's no need. I'm not an alcoholic. Do I enjoy a beer or two? Hell yeah. I'm a fucking rockstar. It's part of my job description.

But I'm not addicted to alcohol. I can go without it. In fact, I have. I haven't had so much as a sip of alcohol since Mercy and I struck our deal. She doesn't want me to drink? I won't drink. Easy peasy.

"Mercy is my girlfriend. Why else would I have had dinner with Old Man Mercury?" I claim.

Jett snorts. "Try again. Everyone here knows you enjoy fucking with crazy people. And Old Man Mercury is as crazy as they come."

My stomach burns at his accusation about Mercy's uncle. "He's not crazy."

"Did you forget about his argument with the gossip gals?" He challenges. "He egged them on in front of the entire town."

"The gossip gals enjoy a good argument."

The gossip gals isn't a derogatory title. The five older women – Feather, Petal, Sage, Cayenne, and Clove who have been dubbed the gossip gals – love the title. They even have t-shirts made up with the name.

"But what about when he—"

Dylan cuts Jett off. "We're getting off track here."

I don't say anything since the track they want to be on is not where I want to be. I don't want to be at the same racing circuit, let alone on the same track.

Cash nods. "Back to the subject at hand."

My bandmates stare at me. If they think they can force me to talk this way, they're wrong. I may have been susceptible to this tactic in the past but not when it comes to Mercy and our relationship. Fake relationship, I correct.

Mercy needs my help to get her uncle moved into a nursing home. I can't let her down. I won't let her down. Based on the hints Mercy made last night, I can guess a lot of people in her life have let her down before. I won't be one of them. I know how it feels to be let down. I have no intention of making Mercy feel abandoned or uncared for.

"I thought we had practice for the tour," I say as I plow through them to get to my closet.

"And I thought you were smarter than this," Cash says.

I snag a pair of jeans and put them on. "I don't know what you mean."

"You know exactly what we mean," Dylan says.

I sniff the t-shirt on the floor and rear back at the smell. Nope. Need another one. I dig through my drawers, grab an old *Cash & the Sinners* concert t-shirt, and slip it on.

"Let's go."

I attempt to herd my bandmates out of the room but they aren't going anywhere.

"Can I at least get a cup of coffee? I have a massive headache." When everyone sighs, I'm quick to add, "I always have a headache the day after an allergy attack."

Jett moves to let me pass and I make my way down the stairs to the kitchen with them hot on my heels. I don't know why I thought getting coffee would be a solo endeavor.

I make a coffee and take a fortifying sip before turning around and leaning against the counter to face them. I'm all out of delay tactics.

"Out with it."

"We're worried about you," Dylan begins. "We know drinking helps you to forget your family."

I growl. "This is not about him."

"Nevertheless, we're worried about how much you've been drinking," Cash says.

I knew this was coming. It's the whole reason I agreed to the charade with Mercy in the first place. I thought – apparently wrongly – if I had a girlfriend, my bandmates would get off my back about my drinking.

"I'm not currently drinking," I say.

Jett points to the clock. "Because it's 9 a.m."

"Weren't we supposed to be at the studio at eight?"

"And now you're dating this girl no one knows about," Cash continues as if I hadn't spoken.

"You've met Mercy. I brought her to the party."

Jett crosses his arms over his chest. "And we're supposed to believe she's your girlfriend? You barely know her. You're giving up our bet for her?"

I shrug. "Maybe I realized our bet is childish."

Fender grunts. It's his favorite means of communication. We didn't dub him grumpapottamus for no reason.

"Fender agrees with me."

Jett rolls his eyes. "And since when do you care what Fender thinks?"

Fender growls.

"I've always cared."

"Didn't stop you from stealing my food," Fender grumbles.

I don't deny it. Before Fender moved in with Leia, he kept our refrigerator stocked. Why would I go grocery shopping when there was plenty of food in the house? Waste of time if you ask me.

"This is bullshit!" Jett yells. "Are you guys not seeing what I'm seeing? He's totally lying about everything! Mercy isn't his girlfriend. And he hasn't stopped drinking."

"I did have to carry him to the car last night," Fender says.

I don't remember him carrying me to the car. At least now I know how I got home last night.

I inhale a deep breath to remain calm. Getting angry won't help matters.

"Because I had an allergic reaction. I wasn't drunk at dinner with Mercy and Mercury. I wouldn't misbehave in front of them."

And I wouldn't. Mercy deserves my respect. Getting drunk and disorderly at a dinner with her uncle would have been totally out of line.

Jett snorts. "Because you would never get drunk and embarrass yourself."

I feel anger well up in my body. How dare he? So much for staying calm. "I didn't say I never get drunk!"

"Because you'd be lying!"

I stomp toward him. "Who do you think you are? You're not exactly a saint."

Dylan shoves his way in between us. "Enough."

I glare at him. He's always Mr. Peacemaker. Sounds boring to me.

"Let's give Gibson a chance to prove he's serious about Mercy and he's done drinking."

I scowl. I didn't say I was done drinking. I'm on a break is all. But I don't contradict Dylan. I don't need these yahoos on my back about my drinking.

"I am," I declare.

Dylan studies me. "He'll go on another date with Mercy soon and then we'll figure out how serious he is."

I need to go out on more dates with Mercy? I thought her showing up at band activities would be enough for these guys.

I glance around the room. Judging by the looks on their faces, it's not. Guess I'm going on a date for the first time in ten years.

Chapter 9

Crossroads – when you are lost and don't know which way to go

MERCY

"Uncle Mercury," I warn. He has the ornery look on his face. It's clear he's about to say something mean.

"What? The place was worse than a drug den."

"How was it worse than a drug den?"

"Did you not notice all the drugs they were handing out? The residents were practically comatose."

I rub my temples where I feel a headache coming on. This is the third nursing home we've visited. None of them were up to my uncle's standards. I'm starting to worry none of them will ever be.

"You're gonna have to choose soon. I can't stay in Winter Falls with you forever."

"Why not?" He asks as I help him into the car. "You got somewhere else to be?"

No. Not exactly. But Winter Falls isn't my home. I need to find a job, a place to live, a life.

"And what about your boyfriend?" Mercury continues as I settle into the driver's seat. "He's in Winter Falls. You're not going to abandon him, are you?"

I wave away his concern. "Gibson travels all the time. And he's rich. He'll visit me wherever I end up."

"What's your rush? Why don't you get a job in town?"

I snort. "I'm a mechanic. There aren't exactly jobs for mechanics in a town where combustion engines are banned."

"Some mechanic you are. You haven't managed to get the piece of junk you drove into town running."

"I don't have any tools. I don't have my shop."

My stomach sours at the reminder of how I no longer have my shop. Of how my ex stole it from me. Such a douchebag. I should have hit him with a wrench when I had the chance.

"Why don't you ask Basil?"

Basil? Basil is a herb not a person. Or?

"Who's Basil?"

"He owns the tow truck in town."

My mouth gapes open. "There's a tow truck in town?"

"Winter Falls is full of surprises."

If there's a tow truck business in town, then I am indeed surprised. I'm also stopping by as soon as we get back in town. Betsy is done for but maybe this Basil guy is interested in buying some parts from her.

I drop my uncle off at the house before steering toward Basil's place. His business is about a mile outside of town on the opposite side of Mercury.

I'm shocked when I pull up to a large garage. It's the first garage I've seen in Winter Falls. There isn't much need for garages when most people use golf carts and bikes to get around. There isn't a sign indicating this is Basil's business but there's a tow truck parked in the driveway.

I open the car door but before I can step out my phone vibrates in my pocket with a message.

Do you want to go on a date tonight?

Why is Gibson asking me out on a date?

Is it a band thing?

Just us.

My brow furrows. Just us? We didn't agree to any dates.

Why?

The band isn't buying we're dating.

Shit. I can't say no now.

What time? I'll meet you.

I'll pick you up at six.

I pause. I don't want him picking me up. I need to keep my distance from the sexy rockstar to remind myself this relationship isn't real. But I can't deny Gibson showing up at the house will help convince Uncle Mercury he's my boyfriend. And maybe pressure him into picking a nursing home.

Okay.

I shove my phone in my back pocket and slam the car door. As I make my way to the garage, the side door opens and a man steps out. I nearly stumble at his appearance. He has long gray hair pulled back in a ponytail. And he's wearing a tie-dye shirt with a pair of bellbottoms.

I wave in greeting.

"You must be Mercy. I was wondering when you'd show up."

My nose wrinkles. "How do you know my name? And why were you expecting me?"

"This is Winter Falls."

I wait for him to continue but apparently he thinks he's answered my questions already. I think not.

"I need more of an explanation."

"You've never lived in a small town before?"

"Nope. I'm from Kansas City."

"Everyone knows everyone's business in a small town."

Bryan said the same thing at the bakery but I didn't believe him. I guess I should have.

"And everyone knows I'm a mechanic?" I haven't been running around telling people what my occupation is.

"Nah. Your uncle told me."

"If this is a set-up for you to give me a job because you owe Mercury a favor, I'm not interested."

"It's not. But I think you'll be interested once you see what I have in my garage." He waves to the building.

Dang it. I am curious. My hands are itching to dive into an engine. I'd even do an oil change for funsies at this point. I'm having withdrawals. I'm used to having my hands on an engine every day. I miss the smell of oil and grease. The puzzling to figure out what's wrong. The touch of steel and iron.

"Lead the way."

He grins. "I knew I was going to like you."

"Yeah, well, I'm a very likeable person."

He chuckles as he shows me into the garage. My jaw drops to the floor at the sight of the classic car in front of me.

"No way," I mutter and run to the Camaro. "What year is she?"

I don't wait for his answer before laying on the creeper and sliding under her. There's a lot of restoration work to be done yet, but the engine looks solid. I roll back out and stand before circling the car.

"Are you doing the upholstery work as well? What about the body work?"

"I have a guy who does the upholstery work, but I do the body as well as the mechanics."

I draw my hand along the blue frame. It's faded and full of rust but the potential is plain to see. "She's a beauty. When did you buy her?"

"She isn't mine."

I pause. "You're restoring her for someone else?"

"Yep." He leans against the wall. "It's how I earn a living."

"Makes sense. I doubt the tow truck business makes much money in this town."

He grunts. "You're not wrong."

I motion to the Camaro. "Is this why Uncle Mercury sent me here?"

"I'm getting old. I can't lift engines the way I used to. And my hands are gnarled. Working with precision is difficult."

"You want to retire?"

"Semi-retire."

I clasp my hands together to hide how they're shaking with excitement. This is the opportunity of a lifetime and I don't want to mess it up. "Do you want to hire someone to help with your restorations?"

He chuckles. "You get straight to the point."

"I have been accused of speaking before thinking a time or two." Or three thousand. Whatever.

"I don't want to hire someone who's going to up and leave after I've got them trained."

I bristle. He doesn't need to train me. I know my way around an engine.

"Are you planning on staying in Winter Falls?"

Good question. I have no idea.

"I don't know. I came to help get Uncle Mercury settled in a nursing home but he's being difficult."

Basil barks out a laugh. "Mercury wants things done his way."

"Trust me. I know."

Who seriously cares which way toilet paper is placed on the toilet roll hanger? Mercury, that's who. I was glad when my ex Zeke remembered to put a new roll on. I never gave a shit about the rest.

"You planning on leaving once Mercury's settled?"

I shrug. I am. Or, I was. But Mercury is right. I don't have anywhere else to be. I didn't think a town full of environmental enthusiasts with a grudge against cars was an option. But maybe it is.

"I guess I'm at a crossroads."

He scratches his chin. "At a crossroads? I know a thing or two about being at a crossroads."

Considering he's dressed like a hippie who doesn't realize the sixties have come and gone, I think he blew past the crossroad and stuck to his path come what may.

"I guess you'll be in town as long as your boyfriend is here at least."

He knows I have a boyfriend in town, too?

"The CIA could follow lessons on spying from the grapevine in this town," I mutter.

"Tell you what. Why don't you come in a few days a week for a few hours? I can get a handle on your skills and you can earn a bit of cash."

I wouldn't sneeze at a bit of extra cash. The sixty-eight dollars in my checking account is going to be wiped out by dinner tonight with Gibson. And I refuse to ask Uncle Mercury for money. I am not a leech. I am not my mom.

"It's a deal." We shake on it and I let him get back to his work.

I smile as I switch on the Charger's engine. I have a job. Maybe I will stay in town a bit longer. I'm not exactly in a hurry to get back to Kansas City where Mom and Zeke are. I could do without seeing either one of them for the rest of my life.

Gibson, on the other hand? I could stare into those light brown eyes for a while. Maybe tug on his hair or lick his tats. My body warms as I imagine exploring all of the many tats Gibson sports.

Whoa. Hold on. Gibson and I aren't really dating. It's a ruse to force my uncle into moving into a nursing home. Nothing more.

Nonetheless, anticipation hums in my blood as I drive back to Mercury's house. I haven't been on a real date in a long time. Picking up takeout Zeke devoured before I had the chance to sit down does not spell date.

I have a feeling Gibson has something else planned for tonight. I can't wait.

Chapter 10

Trouble — can be good or bad but is always fun either way

MERCY

I stare out the window as I wait for Gibson to arrive. I check my watch. It's a few minutes past six. Is he standing me up? Is he always late? Does he think punctuality is for losers?

A golf cart turns into the driveway and I rush to the front door.

"Where are you going?"

Mercury's question has me whirling around.

"I told you. I have a date."

He glowers. "Your young man will come inside to pick you up. You don't go running out the second he arrives."

Is he worried I appear eager? I'm not eager. This isn't a real date.

Except I'm tapping my toes and inching toward the door. Shit. I am eager. I want to see Gibson.

Hold your horsepower, Mercy. This is fake, remember? And I'm on a break from men. Because I can't make good decisions when it comes to them.

"A man should treat a woman properly by coming to the door to pick her up," Mercury says.

I giggle. My uncle doesn't live in the now.

"Men don't come to the door anymore."

He harrumphs. "They should. Having manners isn't old-fashioned."

He's got me there.

Knock! Knock!

Apparently while I've been getting a lecture on manners, Gibson has arrived. I inhale a deep breath and force myself to stroll to the door. I am not eager to lay my eyes on the rockstar's gorgeous face. Not this girl.

"Hi," Gibson smiles and my body immediately leans toward him. The stubble on his chin is now a beard. I want to run my nails over it and watch how he responds.

"Hi." My voice comes out all breathy. I clear my throat and try again. "Hi."

"Good evening, young man," Mercury greets.

Gibson's smile widens. "Good evening, Mercury."

"Ready?" I don't wait for his answer and step forward forcing him to retreat from the door.

Gibson chuckles. "What's the rush?"

I grab his hand and lead him down the stairs to the golfcart. "I fear Uncle Mercury is gearing up to give a lecture on manners in modern day."

"Mercury is a hoot."

We sit in the golfcart and he starts driving us toward town.

"Easy for you to say. You don't live with him. The amount of time the man can spend in the bathroom is epic. And I lived through the great poop incident of 2020."

"The great poop incident of 2020?"

I feel my face heat. Zeke always teased me for using the term poop incident. But when I glance over at Gibson, he appears intrigued. Of course, Gibson isn't my real boyfriend the way Zeke was. Although, is a man really your boyfriend when he's sleeping with every woman within the city limits?

"My ex got salmonella poisoning from eating Chinese take-out. I told him not to order from the place. The restaurant was always a complete mess. Dirty with broken chairs piled in the corner. And the floor?" I do an exaggerated shiver.

"But would he listen to me?" I roll my eyes. "Of course not."

"And thus the great poop incident of 2020."

I nod. "He had diarrhea for a week. It was…"

"I get it. There's only one toilet on the tour bus and five of us. Anytime we order spicy takeout…" He trails off with a mock shiver.

"I cannot imagine living in such close quarters with four other people."

"You don't have any siblings?"

"Nope. It's just me and my mom."

We stop in front of a building and I read the sign *Naked Falls Brewing*. I frown. Is our date at a brewery? I don't drink and he's not supposed to be drinking. The brewery isn't the best choice.

"Um…"

"There aren't any other places in town to eat besides the diner and the brewery," he explains. "And the diner closes early."

"Okay," I give in since he does have a point.

He hurries around the cart and offers me his hand. "Shall we?"

I stare at his hand for a long moment. I should probably avoid touching him since every time we touch I'm tempted to touch him more. Maybe throw myself at him. And I've never been good at resisting temptation.

I grasp his hand and electricity hits me with a whoosh. I nearly stumble but Gibson tightens his hold on my hand to steady me.

"I didn't expect you," he murmurs.

"Expect me? You're the one who asked me out."

"Never mind." He clears his throat. "Shall we?"

I study the brewery as we enter. It has an industrial vibe. The walls are exposed brick and the large ducts are painted a matte black. This place is totally my style.

"You made it," the host greets us.

I glance behind us. He can't mean us.

Gibson frowns. "This is Elder. He's Cash's half-brother."

I wave. "I'm Mercy."

Elder waggles his eyebrows. "Are you going to have mercy on poor Gibson?"

I roll my eyes. "Good one. I've never heard it before."

He chuckles as he leads us up the stairs to a booth in the corner. "This is our date table."

I wait until he's gone before leaning over the table and hissing at Gibson. "Did you tell everyone we're on a date?"

His cheeks darken. "My bandmates know since I'm trying to convince them this is real."

Oh yeah. I forgot this isn't real for a minute. *Head back in the game, Mercy.* You're not falling for another bad boy. Remember how the last one stole all your money?

"I got a job today," I blurt out. Way to be smooth, Mercy.

He lifts his eyebrow. "You did? I thought you were leaving town as soon as Mercury moves into a home."

"I've got nowhere else I need to be." My cheeks warm. Could I be more of a loser?

"Fair enough," he says and relief fills me. "What's the job?"

"I'm a mechanic and I—"

"Hold on," Gibson cuts me off. "You're a mechanic?" I nod. "A car mechanic?"

"Is there any other kind?" My brow wrinkles. "Are you one of those men who think women can't be mechanics?"

He holds up his hand. "No way. Some of our best roadies are women."

"What does a roadie do anyway?"

"Set up and dismantle the stage, take care of the instruments and sound and lighting equipment before and after a show."

"Wow. I didn't realize how tough a roadie job is."

"Yeah, we…" He trails off with a scowl.

"What's wrong?"

He points across the restaurant. I follow his gaze. His bandmates are sitting down at a table on the other side of the room.

"What are they doing here?"

He purses his lips. "They're here to check on me."

Before I can ask him any further questions, the waitress arrives. "What can I get you?"

"Burger and a beer."

I clear my throat. "A beer?"

"It's just one beer."

It always starts with one beer. Or one shot. Or one glass. Spoiler alert: It never stops at one.

"Burger and a coke," I tell the waitress since I don't want her to hear about our 'deal'.

I wait for her to cross the room before I lean forward to hiss at Gibson, "You promised not to drink."

He waves away my concern. "It's one beer."

I frown. "You don't get it. It always starts with one beer. It never ends that way."

"What's the big deal?"

"What's the big deal?" I repeat.

"Yeah." He shrugs. "What's the big deal?"

My anger flares and I forget all about being quiet and putting on a stupid show for his bandmates.

"The big deal is I grew up with an alcoholic mother. Do you have any idea how it feels to be ten and come home from school to clean up your mother's vomit? Or wake up in the middle of the night to check her breathing to make sure she's just passed out and isn't dead?

How it feels for your mom to promise she'll quit time and time again? She's doing good so you bring your friends home to hang out only to discover you mom passed out in her own pee and poop in the living room. And if all those things weren't bad enough, how about the time you bring home a boyfriend and your mom strips off her clothes and tries to seduce him?"

I'm gasping for breath by the time I finish. Gibson reaches across the table for my hand but I shove him away and stand.

"This is over."

I start toward the stairs but he blocks me. "We made a deal."

"And you broke it," I hiss at him.

He squeezes my shoulder. "I won't drink the beer."

I raise an eyebrow. I'm supposed to believe this crap?

"I'll send it back. I promise."

"I don't know you well enough to believe your promises."

"Let's take it day by day," he pleas.

Well, crap. I never can resist a man who begs.

"I don't know," I hedge.

"You want your uncle in a nursing home, don't you?"

Damnit. I forgot all about Mercury. He really does need a nursing home. I can't care for him round the clock. Especially now that I have a job.

Gibson leans closer. "My bandmates are watching us."

Another thing I forgot about.

"I'm going to kiss you now."

What? We didn't agree on any physical contact. Before I have a chance to protest, his mouth meets mine. I expect a quick peck, a brief meeting of the lips.

Instead, Gibson nips at my bottom lip. "Let me in, sassy girl."

"I—"

The second I open my mouth to respond, he takes advantage. He thrusts his tongue into my mouth. His taste of musk with a hint of mint hits me and I'm lost. I moan and he deepens the kiss. I grasp hold of his waist and haul him to me while his hands thread through my hair.

I feel his manhood lengthen and harden against my stomach and my panties dampen in response. I want to throw him down on the floor and have my wicked way with him. Disrobe him and discover all of his tattoos. Touch his naked skin with my hands and my mouth.

Clapping breaks out behind us and I startle. I forgot we weren't alone.

"You're trouble," Gibson murmurs against my lips.

"Right back atcha."

I am in so much trouble. I could barely keep my hands off Gibson before. But now that I've tasted him and felt his hands in my hair, I don't know how I'll resist him.

Like I said. Trouble.

Chapter 11

Spunky – an attitude Gibson can't seem to resist

GIBSON

"How's Mercy doing?" Dylan asks as he plops down on the sofa next to me.

We're sitting backstage waiting for the opening act to finish. I glance at the clock. They started five minutes ago. It'll probably be another hour before we go on.

Usually I fill this downtime with women and booze. I scowl as I glance at the bar in the corner. My fingers itch to grab a beer but I'm not an alcoholic. I don't *need* a drink.

Besides, I promised Mercy I wouldn't drink while we're on tour this week. Considering her past with her mom, I'm not breaking my promise.

I can't believe my sassy girl had such a horrible childhood. I would have never guessed she had wounds she's hiding. I refuse to be another wound she has to carry.

"I'm sure she's fine," I answer Dylan.

"You're sure she's fine or you know she's fine?"

"She's fine," I repeat because I don't know where he's going with this interrogation but he's going somewhere. And the best way to avoid further questioning is to stick to your story.

"How was she doing when you spoke to her today?"

"I haven't…" I trail off when I realize he caught me.

Shit. A *real* boyfriend would phone his *real* girlfriend and not merely fantasize about her. I stand.

"I'm gonna make a call."

I find an empty room. I can always find an empty room wherever the band is. In the past, I used the space to fuck fans. But I don't fuck fans anymore.

"Hey." Mercy sounds breathless when she answers the phone.

"You busy?"

"Mercury insisted I move his chair. He finally let me put up curtains but they don't block the sun enough for him. Apparently, he'll wither and die if the sun touches his skin. I think he's a vampire."

"Vampires don't age."

"Damn. There goes my theory on why he avoids the sun."

I chuckle.

"Shouldn't you be on stage somewhere thrilling fans and making them want to throw themselves at you?"

"Opening act just started."

"Are they any good?"

"Is who any good?"

She huffs. "The opening act. Are they any good?"

"I don't know. Aurora picks a local band wherever we stop."

"Who's Aurora?"

Do I detect a hint of jealousy in her voice? I need to shut this down. I don't do jealous women. I am my own man and I'll do what I want.

But Mercy's jealousy has me smiling. I like this woman. I enjoy her spunk. Her sassiness. I bet she's fun in bed. My cock twitches at the idea. He's ready to explore her sassy mouth.

He's been ready since the kiss in the brewery. The kiss I've imagined while I've been in the shower with my hand on my cock more times than I can count. Those dark red lips would look sexy wrapped around me while she sucks me off.

"Hello! Gibson are you there?"

"I'm here." My voice comes out gruff so I try again. "I'm here. Aurora is the band's assistant."

"Oh."

"Jett's obsessed with her," I blurt out.

"Seriously? Tell me more. Are they having a secret relationship? But everyone knows about it and pretend they don't? Do they have a secret code?"

"They're not having a secret relationship but they want each other."

"Why aren't they involved?"

"Jett doesn't do relationships."

"Why not?"

"It's his story to tell."

"Gotcha."

I wait for her to pry. Women always do. They want to know everything. And once they do, they use all of your secrets against you. I shouldn't have told her about Aurora and Jett.

"Today was my first day working with Basil."

Maybe she won't pry into my life.

"Yeah? How did it go?"

"It was good to get my hands on an engine again. I missed it. We're working on a Camaro now. She's a beauty. I spent the day under her hood working on her."

I wish she'd spent the day under *my* hood working on me. Her hands touching every inch of my skin.

I clear my throat and force those thoughts away. Mercy and I aren't in an actual relationship. And love isn't for me. I've seen how love can turn sour. I'm not interested in experiencing it again.

"And Mercury did okay while you were away?"

She sighs. "He says he was fine but I don't think he drank anything all day. I'm worried he's afraid to go to the bathroom when he's alone."

"What about adult diapers?"

"I am not talking to my uncle about wearing diapers. His pride is hurt enough at how restricted his movements are."

I admire her for respecting Mercury.

"Can you ask for someone to stay with him while you're at work?"

"It's not a bad idea, but I don't know many people in town."

"Why don't you reach out to Indigo?"

"Maybe because the woman keeps declaring herself my new best friend."

I chuckle. "She's harmless."

There's a pause before she whispers, "I've never had many girlfriends before."

My heart hurts for her. She probably didn't have much of a chance to have friends growing up since she was caring for her mother. I grew up with two loving parents. It was all a lie, but I didn't know it at the time.

"Don't you dare pity me," she growls.

"I don't pity you. I wouldn't dare. You'd probably throw a pair of pliers at me."

"Don't be silly." She snorts. "A wrench is way more effective. Heavier, too."

"I guess I better behave."

"Something tells me you never behave."

She's not wrong. But with her I want to behave. I want to follow her rules. I don't want to hurt her. She's been hurt enough.

"What's the fun in behaving?" I tease.

"I have no idea, but everyone's always telling me to behave."

"We can misbehave together," I suggest.

"You don't need me to misbehave."

"No, but it's more fun together."

"Why do I have the feeling you're talking about sex?"

Because I am.

"Caught me."

"You're a bad boy, Gibson…." She pauses. "What's your last name?"

I laugh. "You still haven't googled me?"

"You're obsessed with me googling you."

I'm not obsessed as such. But it would be nice if she knew about the band and our music. And not because being famous is important. I'm a musician. It's in my blood. I want her to at least know about our music even if she claims she'll never enjoy it.

"It's Lewis."

"Gibson Lewis. I'll remember it for when I google you."

"You tease. You're never going to google me, are you?"

"Not when it brings me such pleasure to listen to your voice go up an octave every time you realize I haven't googled you yet."

"My voice doesn't go up an octave."

"What?" She asks in a high voice. "You haven't googled me yet? But I'm rich and famous. I'm a rockstar."

She doesn't give a shit I'm a rockstar. I'm starting to understand why Dylan and Fender fell hard for women who don't care about their fame.

Not that I'm falling for Mercy. I refuse to fall for anyone. But I like Mercy. She's amusing and fun to be around. With a start, I realize I'm missing her. As a friend. I'm missing my friend. I am not falling for her. I refuse.

"Oh crap," she mutters.

"What? What's wrong?"

"Mercury's yelling about the toilet. I bet he clogged it again."

"Do you need me to ring a plumber?"

"I'm a mechanic. I can handle a clogged toilet."

"Have fun."

"I didn't say I'd enjoy it. I should go."

"Don't forget to phone Indigo," I remind her before hanging up.

I pocket my phone. When I saunter into the hallway, Cash, Dylan, Fender, and Jett are waiting for me.

"Why are you smiling?" Jett narrows his eyes on me. "Have you been drinking in there?" He leans close to sniff my breath. "No alcohol."

"Maybe he wasn't alone," Cash suggests, and I scowl. I'm not cheating on Mercy. She deserves better than a man who cheats the second he's away from home.

Dylan grins. "I bet he's been talking to Mercy." Fender grunts. "Fender agrees."

"Don't we need to get on stage?" I walk away, but they follow me.

"He was definitely on the phone with Mercy," Cash says. "Indigo is going to love this."

"Virginia, too," Dylan adds.

"I don't love this," Jett grumbles. "We have a pact."

I'm not breaking our pact to not fall in love but I can hardly tell Jett the truth. The whole point of this charade is to get the band off my back. I may have gotten them off my back about drinking but now they won't stop bugging me about my girlfriend. Having bandmates is exhausting.

I shrug. "Be happy you won our bet."

"What bet?" Aurora asks as she rushes toward us. "Never mind. You're on in five. Are you ready?"

"Someone's bossy," Jett whispers.

"I heard you." Aurora glares at him as she herds us toward the stage. She stops me with a hand on my wrist. "I'm happy for you, Gibson. Mercy sounds wonderful."

"She is."

I nearly stumble when I realize I'm not lying. Mercy is wonderful. She'll make someone a wonderful wife some day.

But not me. I like her. Enjoy her company. Enjoy having a laugh with her. Nothing more. I am not falling for her. I can't chance it.

Chapter 12

Initiation – an excuse to have a girls' night out and interrogate the newcomer for all her secrets

MERCY

I groan when there's a knock on Mercury's door. Today was my second day working with Basil at the garage. I enjoyed it but my muscles are sore. I forgot how physically demanding being a mechanic is.

"Answer the door," Mercury bellows.

"Answer the door, please," I correct.

"What?"

"Have you heard of the word please? It's considered polite."

He snorts. "Never said I was polite."

"No shit."

"Don't swear. It's unbecoming of a woman."

"And it's unbecoming of a man to not use the word please," I insist.

He sighs. "Will you *please* answer the door?"

"I'd love to." I push to my feet.

"Hi!" Indigo greets when I open the door. She's standing on the porch with Virginia and Leia.

"What's happening?"

She beams at me. "It's girls' night."

"Sorry. I can't leave Mercury alone."

She leans around me to shout, "Old Man Mercury, can Mercy come out to play?"

"She's her own woman," he shouts back.

"There. All taken care of."

I step out on the porch and shut the door behind me. "No, it's not," I whisper. "I can't leave him alone. He doesn't drink anything when I'm gone because he's afraid to go to the bathroom alone."

Leia frowns. "She can't leave him. He'll get dehydrated."

"I guess I'll go home." Virginia starts to walk away but Indigo catches her wrist.

"No one's going anywhere and we are having a night out," she insists.

"What about my uncle?"

She smiles. "The solution is already on the way."

"I'm not letting Cayenne in this house," Mercury shouts.

"Seriously?" I shout back. "You have the television blaring all the time but you can hear us when we're whispering on the porch?"

"What did you say?" Mercury pretends he can't hear us.

Leia giggles. "I like your uncle."

"He's my first relative besides my mom and I'm starting to wonder what all the fuss is about having big families," I mutter.

Cayenne, an elderly woman who's sat with my uncle before, bustles up the porch. "I'm here! You go along and have your night out, Mercy." She pats my shoulder as she passes me.

"We'll continue this conversation at my house," Indigo declares.

Relief fills me. I don't have money for a girls' night out since Basil hasn't paid me yet. "We're not going to the bar?"

"Nope. The gossip gals have spies there." Indigo winks.

"Who are the gossip gals?"

"A bunch of elderly women who pride themselves on being busybodies."

"I heard you, Indigo Scott," Cayenne hollers.

I groan. "Do all old people have excellent hearing in this town?"

"I'm not old!" Mercury shouts.

Indigo threads her arm through my elbow. "Let's go. Girls' night waits for no man."

"Which makes sense considering it's a girls' night," Virginia says.

"Buckle up, buttercup. You're not going home to read your book anytime soon," Indigo tells her. "Virginia prefers not to go outside after eight in the evening. She's an eighty-year-old woman hiding in a twenty-nine-year-old's body."

"Preferring to stay at home doesn't make me an old woman."

"Personally," Leia says. "I could do with a break from home before I strangle my twelve going on thirty-year-old daughter."

"We're here." Indigo motions to a Colonial house.

"Wow. Your house is gorgeous."

I'm not trying to flatter her. The house with its green exterior and bright red front door is gorgeous. There's also a wraparound porch complete with a porch swing. I'd love to spend my evenings swinging on the porch relaxing after a long day of work.

"Thank you. It was my grandmother's house."

"My house is down the block." Virginia points to a similar Colonial house a few doors down.

"Do you live on this block, too?" I ask Leia.

"No. I'm on the other side of town in a much more modest house."

Indigo snorts. "More modest house your man doubled in size with an extension."

Leia sighs. "I did try to stop him but do you know how many guitars Fender has?"

Virginia nods. "I can imagine."

Indigo flings the door of her house open. "Welcome!"

"She is way too excited about a girls' night," Virginia mutters.

"Because this isn't any girls' night." Indigo winks. "It's Mercy's initiation."

I back up with my hands in the air. "Initiation? I'm not doing any weird shit like drink blood from a goat's skull."

"Don't be silly. We won't do any weird shit," Indigo insists. "Besides, where would we get a goat's skull?"

"There is the goat farm outside of town," Virginia points out.

I retreat two more steps.

Leia pushes me forward. "They're kidding. Their idea of initiation is bugging you to tell them all of your secrets."

All of my secrets? I can't tell them my secrets. Especially not the one about Gibson being my fake boyfriend. I don't need them tattling to the entire town about how Gibson and I are faking it.

I can't chance Uncle Mercury finding out. He doesn't go anywhere all day long but he somehow knows all the gossip anyway. Until he's settled in a nursing home, this charade must go on.

I plant my hands on my hips. "Is this an interrogation?"

"No, we're here to reassure you," Indigo insists. "You don't need to worry about Gibson cheating on you while he's away, the guys will keep him in line."

Acid burns through my stomach at the idea of Gibson having sex with another woman. I rub a hand over my middle to wipe away the jealousy. I can't be jealous. What Gibson and I have isn't real.

Except I want him. I want to spend days exploring his naked body, licking his skin, memorizing his tattoos. There's something about a man with tattoos that revs my engines. Oh, who am I kidding? There's something about Gibson that revs my engines.

But I am not going to have sex with the rockstar. He practically has the word *player* tattooed on his forehead. I've had enough of players. You can't trust them.

Time to move this conversation along. "I'm more worried he's drinking."

"I can't believe he stopped drinking for you," Leia says. "The guys have been trying to get him to stop forever. You show up and in one swoop he quits."

I shrug. "I wouldn't date him otherwise."

Indigo freezes with her hand in the refrigerator. "Do you have a problem with people who drink?"

"No."

She blows out a breath and pulls a bottle of white wine out.

"But I don't drink."

Her nose wrinkles. "At all?"

"Indigo," Virginia scolds. "When someone says they don't drink, you don't ask them questions. You accept it and offer them a soft drink."

I smile at Virginia. She appears all shy and meek but this woman has a backbone.

Indigo scowls. "You can't tell me you aren't curious."

"It doesn't matter if I'm curious. You're being rude," Virginia accuses.

"It's okay." I'm quick to reassure them. I don't want to be the cause of a fight between them. "I'm used to all the intrusive questions."

Leia barks out a laugh. "You think you've experienced intrusive questions before, but you don't know Indigo. She's the definition of nosy."

"Ah, but was her nickname in school nosy?" I ask.

Leia groans. "Don't tell me we now have two nosy Nellies in our friendship group."

"I never said I was part of this friendship group."

Indigo laughs. "It's cute you think you have a choice."

"Can we at least sit down before you stick your nose in my business?" I ask but don't wait for an answer before plopping down on the sofa. I moan as my muscles relax into the furniture. "This sofa is major comfy. I might sleep here from now on."

Leia's nose wrinkles. "You'll change your mind when Cash bends Indigo over the table and has his way with her in front of you."

Indigo sighs. "For the last time, we didn't realize you were here."

"You need to lock your door."

"Katy Purry needs her freedom."

Virginia shivers. "Her freedom to attack your face while you're sleeping?"

I scan the room. "Where is your cat anyway?"

Indigo shrugs. "Katy Purry comes and goes as she pleases."

"She's probably busy bullying the neighborhood dogs," Leia mutters.

Indigo ignores her and lifts up a bottle of wine. "Is it okay if we drink in front of you?" Before I can nod, she glares at Virginia. "And I'm allowed to ask that question."

I wave away her concern. "It's fine."

"So, you have a problem with Gibson drinking but not us. Interesting."

I chuckle at Indigo's attempt to get me to spill my secrets. This woman doesn't know what the word subtle means.

"My mom's an alcoholic and Gibson is a heavy drinker," I admit.

"Your mom's an alcoholic?" Indigo asks.

I nod.

"I knew we were best friends at first sight."

My brow wrinkles. "You need to explain for the slow kids in the class."

She motions to Leia and Virginia. "We're not just the girl-friends of rockstars. We're also members of the crappy mother club."

"I'll go first." Leia turns to me. "My parents kicked me out when I got pregnant at seventeen."

I gasp. "Where did you go? What did you do?"

"I couch surfed until my grandparents took me in, but my parents have never met my daughter Isla."

"It's their loss," Virginia says. "Your daughter is adorable."

Leia grins. "She's a terror, but I love her more than anything in the world. Don't tell Fender what I said."

Indigo snorts. "Please, Fender loves your daughter as much as you do."

Leia's face softens. "He does."

"I'm next." Indigo sets her glass down on a table. "My mother blackmailed Cash into dumping me at our high school graduation."

"Blackmailed?"

"Yep. She told him she wouldn't pay for my college if he didn't dump me."

"Witch," I grumble. "And I'm not sorry I said your mother is a witch."

Indigo waves away my non-apology. "She is a witch."

"What about you?" I ask Virginia.

"My mother remarried after my father died and the two sons she had with my step-father bullied me, but she refused to believe me when I complained about it."

"It's official." I glance around at the women. "All of your mothers are witches."

"Yours too," Indigo says. I don't deny it since she's right.

My stomach rumbles and Indigo jumps to her feet. "Let's get some snacks."

As the four of us rummage the kitchen for food, a feeling of contentment steals over me. These women understand me. They understand how it feels to have a mother who doesn't support you. To not have family you can turn to in times of need.

I've never had many girlfriends in the past because I've always found it hard to connect with people. But these women could very well become my friends.

Maybe I should stay in Winter Falls.

Chapter 13

Trust – believing your bandmate even when the naked woman is still in the room

GIBSON

I strum my guitar as Cash sings and weaves his magic over the crowd. They sing along and sway with the music as he reaches the end of our hit song *Resurrect.*

I've learned from my mistakes,
I've grown,
And I'll fight for your love,
I've always known,
You're the one I need,
The missing piece of me,
I'm determined to make you see.
I'm gonna win you back,
Prove my love is sincere,
Every moment,
I'll treasure and protect,
With you, I'll resurrect.

As soon as the last note is played, the crowd explodes. I pull out one of my in-ears to listen to the cheers and catcalls and clapping. Nothing gives me a bigger high than the crowd during a concert.

"Good night, Seattle!"

That's my cue. I set my guitar in its rack on the stage before throwing up the devil's horns with both hands and rushing off stage. Jett follows me. Then Fender, Dylan, and finally Cash.

Cash isn't even off the stage before the crowd starts yelling for an encore. We played two hours and I'm soaked in sweat, but I'm pumped up and ready to give them more.

I stroll to our dressing room. Aurora glances up from her phone to nod at me. She frowns at Jett who gives her the finger as soon as she drops her gaze. Those two need to get a room already. An explosion is imminent.

I whip off my t-shirt and throw it on the ground before reaching for a new one. I down a bottle of water as I wait for the rest of the band to put on clean t-shirts.

"How many songs will you play for the encore?" Aurora asks Cash.

"Two."

She scowls. "Five."

He sighs. "This is our last concert. I'm ready to go home."

"You're not going anywhere until tomorrow morning anyway. You have a meet and greet after this."

Now it's Cash's turn to scowl. "Fine, five songs."

I clap my hands together. "Let's go!"

Jett wraps an arm around my shoulders. "At least one of our bandmates can have a girlfriend and still want to play music."

"I want to play music," Dylan says. "But I also want to get home to Ginny."

"I miss Leia and Isla," Fender grumbles.

"Isla sent me a picture of her and Princess." Jett digs his phone out of his bag to show everyone the picture of the little girl with the dog Fender bought her.

Fender snatches the phone from him. "Why is she sending you pictures?"

Jett snatches his phone back. "We're friends."

"I thought you hated children," Aurora says.

He glares at her. "No, just immature women."

She growls and stomps toward him. Dylan steps in her way. "He's riling you up for fun."

She lets out a breath and retreats. "I'm okay."

"You're an asshole," I tell Jett.

"Don't be a sore loser."

I don't give a shit about the bet we had. I don't care about sleeping with a gazillion women. I only want one woman in my bed – Mercy. But I will never sleep with her. She needs a man who knows how to treat her, who will covet her for the prize she is. I am not the man for her. I don't know how to do those things.

"Let's go," Cash hollers.

Despite Cash's grumbling about how long the encore should be, we play seven songs before he signals for us to wrap it up.

I rush off stage with the rest of the band following me. My body is humming, full of energy and adrenaline. I could fly without an airplane right now.

I bounce toward the bar set up in the corner of the dressing room but I don't reach for a beer. I don't need a beer. A coke is fine.

"Meet and greet in five minutes," Aurora shouts.

I lift my t-shirt and sniff it. "I need a shower."

"Make it quick."

I salute her. "Yes, ma'am. Whatever you say, ma'am."

She rolls her eyes and I chuckle. Aurora doesn't take any of our shit.

I grab my bag and make my way to the showers. I strip and step under the water. My cock is hard from the excitement of the concert. I debate giving myself a hand job but decide I don't have time. I step out of the shower but freeze when I realize I'm not alone.

"What the hell are you doing here?" I ask the woman.

In response, she begins to strip off her clothes. She throws her t-shirt on the floor and is left in a shiny pink bra that does nothing to conceal the size of her breasts.

"Whoa!" I hold up my hands and back away. "Not interested."

"There's no need to play hard to get. All the fans know you're always interested in sex with a new woman." She opens up her arms. "Here I am."

"Things have changed." I point to the door. "Please leave."

"Is this a game?" Her eyes spark with challenge. "Do you want me to beg? Maybe get on the floor and crawl to you?"

"No. No. No. I want none of those things."

She points to my still hard cock. "Your mouth says one thing. Your body says another."

I grab a towel and wrap it around my waist. "This has nothing to do with you."

She shrugs. "I don't care who you're hard for."

Is she for real? She'd fuck me even though I'd be thinking of another woman?

"Have some self respect." I step toward the door, but she blocks my escape.

"Oh come on." She massages her breasts. "Don't you want your hands on these?"

The only breasts I want my hands on belong to Mercy. I bet she enjoys it a little rough. Lucky for her, I enjoy rough, too.

The woman places her hand on my chest and I forget all about Mercy. "Do not touch me."

"What's the big deal? You've had sex with half the country by now. Why not add me to the list?"

There is no list. I never kept track of the women I slept with. I used them. Plain and simple. My stomach sours at the thought. I'm an asshole. I need to treat women better.

I grasp the woman's wrist and pull her hand away from me.

The door flies open and Jett stomps inside. "I knew it! I knew you were cheating on Mercy."

"I'm not cheating on Mercy," I grit out. "I'm trying to get rid of this woman without hurting her."

He snorts. "Sure."

"I'm serious. Nothing happened."

"You're naked. She's half-naked and nothing happened? I'm not an idiot. I know you enjoy sex after a concert."

I sigh. Explaining myself to everyone is getting tedious.

"Nothing happened. Can you escort her out of here?"

Instead of helping, he glances over his shoulder and hollers, "Guys!"

Cash, Dylan, and Fender join us.

The woman giggles. "Yippee. I'm getting all of the Sinners tonight."

Dylan picks up her shirt and hands it to her. "Sorry to disappoint but we're not interested."

"She doesn't understand the words not interested," I say.

Cash crosses his arms over his chest. "How about these words? Security is on their way."

She scans the room in confusion but when no one contradicts Cash, she sighs and puts on her shirt before stomping to the door. My bandmates part so she can pass without touching them. Dylan shuts the door behind her.

I drop my towel and begin dressing.

"Aren't you going to say anything?" Jett asks. "He's cheating on Mercy. He'll be back to drinking before long."

I sit on the bench to put on my boots. What I don't do is answer him. He obviously doesn't believe me. It fucking stings he doesn't believe me. This band is my family. It's his family, too. But he doesn't trust me. After all the shit we've been through. Where's the trust?

I stand once I finish dressing and lift up my bag. I start for the door but Jett steps in my path.

"Aren't you going to speak for yourself?"

I drop my bag to square off with him. "I told you several times nothing happened with that woman but you refuse to believe me. What's the use in speaking for myself when you don't listen?"

Dylan taps his chin as he contemplates me. "He's got a point."

Cash nods. "I agree."

"He didn't fuck her," Fender grumbles.

Jett growls. "How do you know? Are you a clairvoyant now?"

Fender shrugs. "He was still hard and the woman was dressed."

"But-but-but," Jett sputters.

"I'm not ruining what I have with Mercy for some faceless fuck."

I'm not lying. I'm not playing a part. I don't want to ruin what I have with Mercy. I rub a hand down my face. Mercy and I aren't a real couple. But she is my friend and I don't want to hurt her. Whether or not we're in a real relationship, it would hurt her if I had sex with a fan.

Cash grins. "Good. I'm glad you're serious about Mercy."

Dylan claps my shoulder. "She's good for you."

Fender grunts in agreement.

I wait for Jett to speak. For him to admit he screwed up.

"This is bullshit," he mutters before stomping off.

Dylan squeezes my shoulder. "He doesn't mean it. He's just reeling because all of us are paired off and he never intends to fall in love."

I frown. I hate lying to Jett. He's my best friend. All the members of the band are my best friends, but I'm closest to Jett.

Maybe I should tell him the truth. What am I thinking? Jett can't keep a secret.

Once Mercy finds a place for Mercury in a nursing home, we can break up. And then things will return to normal.

Except the band will go back to bugging me about my drinking.

Chapter 14

Gossip Gals – Five women who think they're in charge of Winter Falls

MERCY

I've barely had a chance to sit down after I came home from work before there's a knock on the door.

"I know. I know," I say and stand before Mercury can speak. "I'll get it."

"If it's your girlfriends, keep the noise down," he orders.

Whatever.

"Hi, Cayenne," I greet as I open the door. "I didn't know you were coming by today." I glance at the four elderly women standing on the porch with Cayenne. "With your friends. Can I help you?"

"We're here to help you," one of the women says as she pushes her way past me inside the house.

"Maybe you can introduce yourself before you barge inside," I grumble.

Uncle Mercury scowls and stands. "I'll be in my bedroom."

"How do you know these women didn't come here to see you?" I holler after him.

"Don't care!"

"He can be a bit persnickety," I say in way of an apology.

"Don't you worry. We know how Mercury is."

"We've known him for fifty years."

"And we're not here for him."

I motion to the living room. "Have a seat. What are you here for? And what are your names? I can't keep referring to you as old lady number one and old lady number two in my head."

My eyes widen when I realize I called them old to their faces. Oops.

"She's not wrong. We are old," Cayenne mumbles.

"I'm Sage," the bossy one declares. "I'm the leader of the gossip gals."

"The gossip gals?" Indigo mentioned the gossip gals before but I thought she was joking.

Cayenne smiles. "Has a certain ring to it, doesn't it?"

Sage clears her throat. "You've already met Cayenne. The others are Feather, Petal, and Clove."

I wave to them. "Hi."

"I like her. She says what she's thinking," Clove says.

"Most people don't enjoy how I say what I'm thinking."

"Most people are boring," Feather says. "Do you read sexy books?"

What an abrupt change of topic, but I roll with it. "If the hero is a cowboy or a vampire or a shifter, I'm in."

Feather rubs her hands together. "We haven't had a cowboy hero for a while." She opens her bag and removes a kindle.

"Are we going to read together?"

"Don't be silly," Sage says. "She's searching for the next book for our sexy book club."

"You run a sexy book club?"

Winter Falls keeps getting more and more interesting. Who knew a small town would have a sexy book club run by a bunch of people old enough to be my grandma? Sign me up.

"Technically, Aspen runs it," Clove answers.

"Who's Aspen?"

I haven't met many people who live in town besides the members of the band and their girlfriends. I'm mostly stuck in the house with Mercury when I'm not working. It's a change of pace from going out to a bar most nights after work with the crew from the garage, but I'm enjoying the quiet life. For now, at least.

Feather glances up from her e-reader. "She owns the bookstore, *Fall Into A Good Book.*"

I didn't know there was a bookstore in town. I really have been living a sheltered life since I arrived in Winter Falls.

"You'll meet her at the next book club," Sage declares as if me attending book club is a done deal.

"Assuming you're still in town," Clove adds.

I chuckle. "No one's ever accused you ladies of being subtle, have they?"

"They wouldn't know subtle if it came up and bit them in the ass," Mercury shouts from his room.

"Why didn't you stay in the living room if you're going to listen to our conversation?" Sage yells her question toward the hallway.

"I don't need no old ladies interfering in my life," he shouts back.

"But it's okay for them to interfere in my life?"

Naturally, Mercury doesn't respond to my question. Suddenly, he can't hear. Oh, please.

Petal bats her eyelashes. If she's trying to appear innocent, it's not working. "Why do you think we're interfering in your life?"

They're totally here to interfere with my life. I just don't know how yet. "One, you said you're here to help me. Two, you've dubbed yourself the gossip gals."

Sage smiles. "I like her."

"This is going to be my favorite project," Petal declares.

"I'm not a project. I'm not going to be the subject of a makeover. What you see is what you get." I lift up my foot and twirl it around to show off my cowboy boot.

"We wouldn't dream of doing a makeover on you. You're quite adorable as you are," Feather says.

"Adorable enough for a man to fall in love with," Clove adds.

I hold up my hands. "Whoa. Hold up, buttinsky gang. I'm not planning on falling in love with anyone."

"What about Gibson? You are dating him, aren't you?" Sage asks with a flutter of her lashes.

I narrow my eyes at her. Does she know the truth? Judging my the sparkle in her eyes she knows something.

"We are dating, but we're taking things slow."

Feather's nose wrinkles. "You haven't had sex yet?"

I bark out a laugh. "No, we haven't had sex, Ms. Meddle-some."

Pleasuring myself while imagining Gibson naked above me doesn't count no matter what my mother says.

Cayenne leans forward. "Aren't you worried about him getting tempted and having sex with a groupie while he's gone?"

I wasn't since Indigo assured me the rest of the band would keep him in line. But now I am.

I hate cheaters. Zeke was a cheater but no matter how many times I accused him of stepping out on me, he denied it. Until I caught him red-handed in our bed with two other women. I bet they were mighty disappointed at the end of the night. Especially after I stole their clothes and shredded them.

"I'm confused. Do you want me to fall in love? Or do you want me to break up with Gibson? You're sending mixed messages."

"They want to matchmake you with Gibson," Mercury says from the mouth of the hallway.

"Did you get tired of shouting?" I ask as I stand to help him.

He bats me away. "I can stand on my own."

I cock an eyebrow. "You're using a cane."

"A cane doesn't count."

I open my mouth to argue with him – I can argue until the cows come home and often do – but I remember we're not alone. I snap my mouth shut and return to my place on the sofa.

"Mercury," Sage scolds. "You're not supposed to tell her she's our next project."

"I hate to disappoint you but you already told me I'm your next project," I remind her.

She purses her lips. "But you're not supposed to know it's a matchmaking project."

"You've mentioned my boyfriend several times."

"This is fun," Petal declares. "No one ever contradicts Sage."

"I'm not trying to be contrary."

Mercury barks out a laugh. "It comes natural to you. Your grandmother Lyra was contrary, too."

"How was she contrary?" I ask.

Uncle Mercury hasn't told me much about my family despite my numerous questions. He always puts me off with promises of *later*. Guess what? Later has arrived.

"If Adhara said the weather was lovely, Lyra would put on a sweater and complain it's cold."

I smile. "I think I would have liked Lyra."

"You never met your grandmother?" Clove asks.

"Nope. Grandma kicked Mom out of the house when she got pregnant with me. Mom hated her and wouldn't let me see my grandmother. By the time I was old enough to find my grandmother for myself, she'd already passed away."

"Good." Sage nods. "We did the right thing."

I narrow my eyes on her. "What did you do?"

I expect her to lie or come up with some fib. To my surprise, she answers. "We phoned your mom and told her about her uncle needing help."

"We also might have told her she'd need to sell his house," Petal adds.

Now it all makes sense. My greedy parent strikes again. Mom thought she'd get the money from the sale of her uncle's house. I'm surprised she didn't come here herself and force Mercury into a home.

Wait. I'm not surprised. She's always been lazy.

"Welp." Sage stands. "I think we've overstayed our welcome."

"You weren't welcome to start with," Mercury grumbles. "And no matchmaking my niece."

"Is everyone forgetting I already have a boyfriend?"

No one answers as the rest of the gossip gals stand and follow Sage to the door.

Feather pats my hand as she passes me. "And don't you worry about Gibson. I'm sure he was good while he was on tour."

"Those ladies are up to something," Mercury says once I close the door.

They definitely are but I'm not sure what. If they want me to stay with Gibson, why do they keep bringing up the possibility of him cheating? Do they want me to break up with him because they have another man picked out for me?

Not happening. I'm not dating anyone but Gibson. He's the only man who's caught my eye since I found out my ex was cheating. The only man to cause me to question my decision to take a break from men. The only man I think about when I'm naked in the shower.

I blow out a breath and force my thoughts away from Gibson in the shower.

This relationship is fake. Gibson and I are not dating. As soon as we both get what we want from the situation, it'll be over.

I ignore how my stomach sours at the reminder. I must be hungry is all.

Chapter 15

Kiss – the second best way to stop a woman from shouting at you

GIBSON

"Anxious to see Mercy?" Dylan asks as we drive back to Winter Falls.

We finished a week of concerts and are on our way back home. I thought the idea of doing little concert tours a week at a time was weird when Cash and Dylan suggested it, but it's actually nice to get a break. Playing seven shows in seven days is exhausting.

"Why do you ask?"

Dylan nods to my knee. Huh. I didn't realize it was bouncing.

"He's not anxious to *see* Mercy. He's anxious to *do* Mercy," Jett jokes.

I glare at him. "Don't talk about Mercy that way."

Jett groans. "Are you going to be boring now, too? Since you've fallen in love?" He feigns retching.

"I'm not in love."

"Sure, you're not."

I'm not. I like Mercy. She's cool and fun. But in love?

I open my mouth to deny being in love again but I'm supposed to be dating Mercy. Do people who are dating want to fall in love?

I don't want to fall in love and get married. I've seen what it does to people. No thanks.

"I thought you were off to San Diego for the surfing competition?" I ask since I'm done discussing me and love.

"I need to pick up my gear and then I'm out of here." He checks his watch. "My flight leaves in a few hours."

"Why didn't you ask Aurora to handle your gear? It would have saved you a flight."

He scowls and glances away.

I chuckle. Jett's easy to tease when it comes to Aurora. Those two need to get a room already.

"Home," Fender grumbles as he parks in front of his house.

Leia, Indigo, and Virginia are standing on the porch waiting for us. I feel a twinge of disappointment when I realize Mercy isn't with them. But then the door opens and there she is.

She's wearing a short skirt with her cowboy boots. My eyes hone in on those bare legs. They appear a mile long. I want those toned legs wrapped around my waist while I pound into her. My cock twitches in agreement.

I start to smile but stop when she scowls at me. Why is she scowling? What's wrong?

I jump out of the Hummer and hurry to Mercy. Her scowl deepens as I approach. "What's wrong?"

"Is that anyway to greet your girlfriend?" Indigo asks.

I ignore Indigo and shackle Mercy's wrist before dragging her off the porch and across the yard to my house next door.

"What's going on?" I ask once we're behind closed doors.

She crosses her arms over her chest. "Why didn't you tell me about the woman?"

My brow wrinkles in confusion. What is she talking about? "What woman?"

She shoots daggers out of her eyes at me. "What woman? Are you going to deny you had a naked woman with you in the shower?"

"Oh, her."

"Oh, her? That's your response?"

I hear a bag of chips open up and glance over my shoulder. Jett is sitting on the sofa with a beer and chips. "What are you doing?"

"What does it look like? I'm enjoying the show." He motions to us. "Please proceed."

"Don't you have a surfing competition to get to?"

He shrugs. "I'll grab a later flight."

I point to the door. "Out."

He sighs as he stands. "You're no fun anymore."

I am not arguing with him about this. I march to the door and fling it open. He gathers his stuff and heads for the door.

"Try not to get bitten by a shark this time."

"Try not to fall in love and break our pact," he growls at me as he leaves.

"Have a good time!" Mercy hollers after him. He flicks a hand at her.

I shut and lock the door before returning to her.

"Now, where were we?"

She rolls her eyes. "You were acting as if a naked woman in your shower wasn't a big deal."

"It wasn't a big deal."

"I can't deal with this. I can't deal with a cheater. I've had enough of men cheating on me. Consider our deal over."

She stomps toward the door but I hurry to stand in front of her to block her.

"I did not cheat on you," I grit out.

She leans forward to get in my face. "Just because this is fake doesn't mean you didn't cheat on me."

"I didn't cheat on you because nothing happened with the woman. How did you even find out about it?"

"Seriously? You're more concerned about getting caught than with how you hurt me." She scowls. "Typical man."

I growl. "I am not a typical man."

She stabs me in the chest with her finger. "Yes. You. Are."

I grasp her hand. "I am not."

"You think you're so special because you—"

I've had it. I slam my mouth to hers before she can continue. She gasps and I thrust my tongue inside. She tastes spicy with a hint of coffee and chocolate. I love spicy things.

I stroke my tongue into her mouth. I don't know what I'm expecting Mercy to do. Fight me? Claw at me? She does none of those things. Her tongue meets mine and she tries to push into my mouth. I don't think so.

I growl and thread my hands through her hair to angle her head so I can deepen the kiss. Our tongues dual for supremacy while her hands grab hold of my shoulders and pull me closer.

I press my hard length against her stomach and she moans down my mouth. When she lifts her leg and wraps it around my waist, I grab hold of it and hitch it higher until my cock pushes against her core. She groans and rubs herself against me.

I rip my mouth from hers. "You need something, sassy girl?"

She nods.

"What do you need?"

Her eyes narrow. "You know what I need."

I raise an eyebrow. "I do?"

"You're an asshole."

"I'm an asshole who can make you see stars."

She snorts. "You're a walking, talking cliché. The rockstar can make me see stars."

I lift her up and she wraps her legs around me. We fit together perfectly. Her breasts rub against my chest. Her mouth is level with mine. Perfect.

I whirl around and slam her against the wall. She gasps and her eyes sparkle with excitement. My sassy girl enjoys it a bit rough. Good. Since I prefer it a bit rough myself.

"Starting to get the picture?" I whisper into her ear before biting on her earlobe.

She arches her back and her head falls back. It hits the wall with a thud but she doesn't appear to notice as she writhes in my arms.

I've never been with a woman who's this responsive to me. It's exhilarating. And tempting. How far can I push her?

"I'm going to fuck you right here against this wall next to my front door."

"I dare you."

Hell yeah. This woman is my match. Sassy and challenging to her core. Things I've always hated in other women but with her I get off on them.

"Take me out," I demand.

She reaches between us and unsnaps my jeans. She doesn't wait before lowering the zipper and shoving her hand inside my boxers.

She wraps her hand around my cock and squeezes. I groan and thrust into her hand. She pumps up and down my length. Her hand isn't soft or tentative. She's bold and demanding. I grit my teeth before I come. I'm not coming until I'm buried deep inside her pussy.

"Lift up your skirt and put me inside you."

"Make me."

I nip her chin. "Put me inside you and I'll make you come."

She bites her bottom lip as she considers it. "I can make myself come."

My cock twitches and she grins.

"I'm watching you make yourself come while you're spread out on my bed. But first I'm fucking you against this wall." Her breath hitches and I feel her hard nipples press against my chest.

"Now lift up your skirt and put me inside you." I pause. "Or do you want me to punish you for not behaving?"

Her brown eyes darken until they're nearly black. She's intrigued. Perfect for me.

I growl. I need in her now. "Lift. Your. Skirt."

She stares into my eyes as she lifts her skirt ever so slowly.

"Reach into my back pocket and pull out my wallet." As much as I want into her bare, I need to get checked first. I will never risk Mercy. Not her.

I wait until she has the wallet in her hand. "Pull out a condom and put in on me."

She rips the packaging open and slides the condom on me.

"Now push your panties to the side and put me inside you."

She places my cock at her entrance. I push inside an inch.

"Fuck. You're soaked for me."

"And you're hard for me," she sasses.

"I'm going to fuck you now."

"Promises, pro—"

Her words break off when I sink into her. I thrust until my balls slap against her skin. I have to pause before I come. She feels good. Too good to believe.

Her walls ripple around me.

"Feel good?" I ask but don't wait for an answer before slowly withdrawing. I enjoy the feel of every inch of her pussy until merely my tip remains inside.

"Ready?"

"Yes," she moans.

I slam into her and her fingers dig into my shoulders. I can feel the prick of her nails beneath my t-shirt. Next time we'll be naked. But there's no stopping to remove our clothes now.

"Harder," she demands.

I pound into her as she holds on for the ride. It isn't long before I feel my balls grow heavy with the need for release. But I'm not coming before her.

Her walls tighten around me. Thank fuck.

"You gonna come for me, sassy girl?"

She glares at me and I realize we've been staring into each other's eyes the entire time I've been inside her. I can't help it. She mesmerizes me. I'm enthralled with her and I don't think I want to escape her snare.

"I'll come when I…"

I angle my hips to hit her clit and she gasps.

"You'll come now," I demand.

Her breath hitches and she grunts.

"Don't hold back, sassy girl. Give it to me."

I increase my pace and she moans as her walls attempt to strangle me.

"Gibson," she growls as her climax hits.

I let go and pound into her. My rhythm is erratic as I chase the finish line.

"Mercy, Mercy, Mercy," I chant as I come.

I glide in and out of her until our climaxes wane. Her eyes close and she slumps against the wall.

"I needed that."

I grin. "We've barely begun."

Her eyes snap open. "More?"

I kiss her nose. "Lots more."

Chapter 16

Busy day – when you kick yourself out of your own bed

GIBSON

I smile as I wake. I'm cuddled up to a warm body. A warm body I woke several times in the middle of the night to have my wicked way with. Mercy was a more than willing participant.

Mercy?

Shit. I fucked things up again. This is supposed to be fake. I don't want a real relationship. Relationships end up with people using you. Exploiting you. I can't risk it.

I unwind my arm from around Mercy's waist and inch to the edge of the bed. When she rolls over and snuggles into the pillow, I climb out. I quickly dress before tiptoeing out of the room.

I step onto the porch and scan the area. What am I going to do now?

This is why I kick women out of my bed after sex. There are no awkward mornings after where I end up standing outside my house wondering where I can hide until the woman in my bed gets the hint and leaves.

But I can't kick Mercy out of my bed. She's supposed to be my girlfriend. Good thing Jett's not around to watch this play out.

I shiver. October in Winter Falls is chilly. I need a nice cup of coffee to warm me up. And maybe some pastries. *Bake Me Happy* it is.

"What are you doing here?" Bryan asks the second I open the door.

I glance behind me but there's no one there. "Me?"

"Yes, you. Mr. Rockstar who arrived home last night. You should be cuddled up in bed with your girlfriend." He narrows his eyes on me. "Unless you and Mercy had a fight."

I wag my finger at him. "Nuh-uh. You aren't getting any gossip from me."

"No fair," he pouts.

"Can I get a coffee and a muffin?"

"Don't you mean two coffees and two muffins?"

"You're incorrigible."

He grins. "But oh so much fun."

I pay and settle at a table away from the window to eat my muffin and drink my coffee in silence. My phone buzzes in my pocket. Good. A distraction. I could use one from the thoughts running through my mind about Mercy and how I messed everything up.

"Hey, Rob," I answer the phone.

Rob is the studio engineer of *Bertie's Recording Studio*. *Bertie's* is the studio here in Winter Falls where we recorded our last album. Although the album's finished, I haven't left town yet. Winter Falls is as good a place as any to avoid my parents.

"I know this is last minute, but can you fill in as a session guitarist today?" When I don't answer, he goes on. "I know asking a musician in a big name band to be a session guitarist isn't usually done, but where am I going to find a guitarist of your caliber in Winter Falls?"

I chuckle. "It's fine. I'll do it."

"You will?"

I don't have anything better to do. And this will help me avoid my house and Mercy for a little longer.

"When do you need me?"

We make arrangements and I hang up. I'm shoving my phone into my pocket when Bryan sets a plate of pancakes on my table.

"You're going to need your energy today."

"You're not even going to pretend you weren't listening in?"

He shrugs. "I am who I am."

He skips away and I dig into my pancakes.

When I finish my breakfast, I stroll across the street to the studio. Everything is close in Winter Falls. I thought it would be stifling when we came to this tiny town in Colorado to record our album, but I'm kind of digging how close everything is. How the residents protect us from fans to allow us to live our lives.

"Holy crap," a man swears when I enter the studio. "It is Gibson Lewis. I thought Rob was pulling our legs."

"Always trust your engineer," I say as I extend my hand.

"I'm Simon." He pumps my hand up and down with a smile on his face. "Gibson Lewis. You're Gibson Lewis of *Cash & the Sinners.*"

"I'm gonna need my hand back if you want me to play."

"Oh right." He drops my hand and motions to the other men in the reception area of the studio. "This is Beck, Adam, and Bruce. Beck plays keyboard. Adam is our bass player. And Bruce is our drummer."

Their mouths gape open as I shake their hands. I get them being starry-eyed. I was the same way when *Cash & the Sinners* first hit it big and I met some of my favorite musicians.

But I'm in no mood to stand around and chat. My fingers itch for my guitar. Spending the day playing is a surefire way to get Mercy out of my mind.

"Shall we get to work?" I lead them toward the studio. We enter the control room and Rob greets me.

"Thanks, man. I owe you. I'll send a case of beer over to your place."

I grimace. Mercy will lose her mind if she finds out I have beer. But I'm not going to drink it. No matter how much my mouth waters at the idea. As long as Mercy and I are in a fake relationship, I agreed not to drink.

Of course, I also agreed the relationship was fake and we wouldn't have sex. I broke the hell out of the no sex rule yesterday and last night. And this morning.

Why does every thought lead back to Mercy?

I stick my hands in my pockets. "I had the day off anyway."

"And Mercy's working?"

I groan. I should have known Rob's tapped into the gossip chain in this town. The band brought him here for our album but he decided to stay when the studio offered him a permanent position.

"Did you get my guitar?"

I'm happy to fill in as a session musician today but I will not play any other guitar than my own. Lucky for me, Fender built a studio in his backyard where he stores my guitars.

Rob nods to the studio where three of my guitars are standing in racks.

I lift my chin in thanks before proceeding into the studio. The band is already in there getting ready.

"First album?" I ask when I notice how jittery they are.

"Yeah." Simon beams.

I strap on my guitar and quickly make sure it's tuned. Once I'm ready, I nod to him.

"Shall we play through the song a few times before we start recording?" He asks.

"Sounds good."

Bruce counts us off with his sticks and we begin. The song isn't bad. It's not *Cash & the Sinners* level. Not yet. But it isn't bad.

"Can I make a few suggestions?" I ask once we finish the first run through.

Simon glances around his band for confirmation before answering me. "Sure."

"The bridge here could use a bit of cleaning up. Maybe switch the key?"

We work on some changes to the song for a while. When we have the changes nailed down, Simon smiles.

"The song is way better now."

Beck snorts. "I'm surprised you let anyone make any changes to your precious song."

"Control freak," Adam mutters.

"I am not a control freak," Simon argues.

Bruce barks out a laugh. "Said by every control freak in the world."

"I'm not that bad."

Beck rolls his eyes. "You walked out of a discussion with one producer because he wanted to make changes."

"Those weren't changes. It was an entirely new song."

"Control freak," Adam mutters again.

"Can you guys at least pretend to be professional in front of Gibson?" Simon urges.

I wave away his concern. "No worries. If a band isn't razzing each other, it's falling apart."

"You want to record some time today?" Rob asks over the microphone. "Gibson's time is precious."

I nearly roll my eyes. I don't exactly have anything else I need to do today.

"Oh shit. Sorry. Let's do this," Simon says and everyone nods in agreement.

We play the song for hours. Sometimes you play a song once and it's ready. Sometimes you need to play it for days until you get it just right. Considering this band is new to recording, I'm not surprised when it's after five before Rob finally says he's happy with the sound.

"Awesome!" Simon shouts and the rest of his band join him.

"Let's go party," Beck suggests.

"Where is there to party in this town?" Adam asks and everyone glances my way.

"You can go to the brewery, *Naked Falls Brewing*. It's next door. Or there's the bar, *Electric Vibes,* at the end of the block."

Bruce jumps up from his stool behind the drums. "I vote bar."

"Second!" Adam shouts.

"You coming?" Simon asks as they approach the door.

I shake my head. No partying for me.

"No?" Simon's brow wrinkles. "But you're a legendary party maker."

I *was* a legendary party maker. Before Mercy. I don't want to ruin things with her by tying one on. I promised her I wouldn't drink and I will keep my promise. No matter how much I'm dying to have a beer.

"I'm good."

Bruce chuckles. "He's probably going to pick up a chick and lose himself in her for a few hours."

"Yeah," Beck agrees. "The man is a legend."

I am not picking up another woman. I don't want any woman other than Mercy. My breath catches in my throat when the thought penetrates.

I don't want any other woman than Mercy.

Shit. I'm falling for my sassy girl.

This is a bad idea. I know what love does to people. It makes them believe they have rights to you.

No. Mercy's different. She would never try to use me. And she doesn't care about my money.

I hope.

Chapter 17

Lightening strike – how it feels to get the surprise of a lifetime

MERCY

I groan as I wake up. My body aches in places it hasn't ached in a long time. In places it's never ached before. Gibson knows how to make my body sing. And he did over and over last night.

I roll over to wish him good morning but his side of the bed is empty. I listen for any sounds in the house but it's quiet.

"Gibson!" I call, but there's no reply.

Did he leave me alone in his house? What the hell?

I pound my fist against the mattress. I'm such an idiot. Of course, he took off. He warned me enough times how he isn't interested in a relationship or love.

I should give him a piece of— The time on the bedside clock catches my attention. Damn. I'm late for work.

Gibson's lucky I'm late because otherwise I would snoop through all of his things. And I do mean *all of his things.* Drawers, closets. You name it and I'd snoop through it. How dare he run away after the night we shared.

The night we shared? This is fake, Mercy. Fake. Fake. Fake. But it sure felt real last night when Gibson whispered sweet nothings into my ear while he moved inside me. When we stared into each other's eyes as we came together.

It felt magical. Another reminder magic doesn't exist.

I get out of bed and search the floor for my clothes. My panties are ripped beyond repair, so I throw them in the trash in the bathroom.

If Gibson expects me to chase after him, he's going to be sorely disappointed. I'm done chasing after men. It's time they chased me instead.

Enough of this stupid contemplation about a man who will use my body but doesn't want me. I need to get to work and stop standing here thinking up ways to get my revenge on Gibson.

I hurry to the town hall where there are golfcarts residents are free to use. I hop on one and drive as fast as I possibly can to Basil's garage. Which isn't very fast. I bet I could tinker with this engine and make it faster.

When I pull into the garage, Basil steps out and crosses his arms over his chest as he waits for me. Thoughts of tinkering with the golfcart engine evaporate as I rush to him.

"I'm sorry I'm late. I'm usually on time."

He looks me up and down and chuckles. I squirm as he takes in the clothes I wore yesterday. "If I had remembered your boyfriend's band returned from their tour yesterday, I would have told you to take the day off."

Busted. I feel my cheeks warm, but I power through it. "Don't you worry. I'm young. I can work all day after a few hours of sleep."

"A few hours of sleep? I need to talk to your man. He shouldn't have let you sleep at all."

I slap his shoulder. "You're a menace."

He waggles his eyebrows. "I may not be young anymore but I'm still fun."

"I bet you are." I motion to the garage. "Shall we get to work?"

He clears his throat. "Actually. I have something to discuss with you first."

"Are you firing me for being late one time? I promise it won't happen again."

"I'm not firing you for being late."

"I already apologized for having to redo the paintjob. I didn't realize the paint was still wet." Good thing I was wearing overalls because blue automotive paint doesn't come out of jeans. Ask me how I know.

He scratches his chin. "Why do you think I'm going to fire you?"

"Because nothing ever goes well for me for very long and the downfall has already begun." I snap my mouth shut before I admit Gibson ran out on me this morning. The town is too interested in our relationship as it is.

"Nothing ever goes well for you for very long?"

"Nope. Did I not tell you about the time I built up this great business and thought things were going awesome? But then I found out my boyfriend was cheating. And when I left his ass I discovered my name wasn't on any of the business documents and I had nothing? Not even a job when my ex fired me?"

"Your ex sounds like an asshole."

"He sounds like an asshole because he is one. He's also a sucky mechanic. I bet the business is failing without me there."

Not to brag or anything but the customers came for me. Not for him. Which would have been hard since he was always taking off for 'house calls'. House calls my ass. He was sleeping his way through Kansas City.

Basil pats me on the shoulder. "You're better off without him."

"Damn right I am."

"And Gibson seems good for you."

I narrow my eyes at him. "Are you seriously trying to get gossip out of me? Are you a member of the gossip gals?"

"Since I'm a man, no."

"But you are trying to get the gossip."

He shrugs. "I'm an old man. I need to live vicariously through someone."

I snort. "I'm not blind. I saw the woman sneaking out of your house the other day."

He grins. "Never said I was a monk."

"Obviously not, you dog you."

"Anyway, let's have a seat in my office. I have a proposition for you."

"I won't do anything for less than a million dollars," I quip.

He shakes his head as he leads me to his office. I study the room when we're inside. I've never been in here before. It's a mess. There are papers piled everywhere. There's also a carburetor on the desk leaking oil on the papers there.

I motion toward the filing cabinets. "Maybe you should buy more of those."

His chair squeaks as he sits in it. "Have a seat."

The only other chair in the place is piled high with paperwork. I lift the pile up and set it on the floor. "Have you seriously never filed a piece of paperwork in your life?"

He shrugs. "Paperwork is for pencil pushers."

I'm not much for paperwork myself. I'd rather work with my hands.

"What do you want to discuss?"

He leans back in his chair. "I want you to take over the business."

My nose wrinkles. "What business? This business?"

He nods.

"But you barely know me."

"I know enough. I know you're a hard worker. I know you're a damn fine mechanic."

"It's true. I am a damn fine mechanic."

He chuckles. "And modest, too."

"Being modest will get you nowhere when you're a woman working in a man's field."

"I don't have any experience but I expect you're right."

"Trust me. I am. It happens more often."

"So, what do you say? You want to take over my business?"

"The tow truck business?" I ask since he can't possibly mean his renovation business.

"All of it. The tow truck. The car renovation business. The garage. Everything."

"Yes!" I shout. "I'd love, too." I'm already thinking about how I can celebrate when I remember. I have no money. Sixty-eight dollars won't exactly buy me a business. "But I can't afford to."

He waves away my concern. "Ask your uncle for a loan. I'm sure he'll give you one."

"But he needs his money to pay for a nursing home. I don't want him in one of those government ones where the nurses chain the wheelchairs to the wall." I have no idea what government nursing homes are like, but I'm not chancing it.

"Ask him. He can afford it."

"Is my uncle rich or something?" I joke but Basil doesn't laugh. His gaze on me is steady. "Shit. You're not joking."

"Nope."

Uncle Mercury's rich? Why is he living in a house in need of serious repair if he has money? Why does he wear clothes worn clear through? We're having a talk later today.

"Anyway, you'll need approval from the town to take over the business."

I hold up a hand. "Hold on. I jumped in with both feet without thinking again."

"What's there to think about?" He narrows his eyes on me. "Unless you're planning to leave Winter Falls."

I scratch my neck. I actually haven't made up my mind one way or another about Winter Falls. I enjoy living here. I've made friends. The town is a freaking hoot with all of its festivals and unique shops.

And I have no interest in returning to Kansas City where everyone knows Zeke was cheating on me. And where my mom lives. I'm surprised she hasn't been blowing up my phone asking where the money from the sale of Mercury's house is.

"I'm staying," I declare. There's no point hemming and hawing over a decision. Staying feels right in my gut, so I'm staying.

"The next town business meeting is in two days. You can present your proposal to takeover the business then."

My mouth gapes open. "Two days? How do you expect me to put together a presentation in two days?"

I wouldn't even know where to begin. I haven't given a presentation since high school. And somehow I don't think the business people of Winter Falls will be impressed with my presentation on the brown antechinus and how the male can have sex for up to fourteen hours at a time during mating season.

"You'll be fine." He stands. "Now, let's get to work."

"But we haven't even discussed how much I'll pay you for the business and the garage and the tow truck."

My heart speeds up until breathing becomes difficult. Even if Uncle Mercury lends me the money, it's going to be a lot. And I'll have to pay it back. Maybe I shouldn't buy the business. Maybe I should stay in my lane.

Basil rubs my shoulder. "Calm down, Mercy. Everything will be fine in the end."

"And if it's not fine, it's not the end?"

"Exactly."

I inhale a few deep breaths to get my breathing under control and stand. I am not a simpering woman who stumbles at the first obstacle. I will get a loan. I will get approval from the town. And I will make this business a success. Car collectors will fight for my services.

Just you wait and see.

Chapter 18

Foot – despite its size can get lodged in the mouth

MERCY

"Are you sure about this?" I ask Uncle Mercury as I help him up the stairs at city hall. The town business meeting is tonight and my nerves have me shaking in my cowboy boots.

"Mercy Keller, are you doubting yourself?"

I grimace. "It's a lot of money."

"It's my money and I'm giving it to you."

I freeze on the steps. "No, you're lending it to me."

"I'm giving it to you, and my decision is final."

I cross my arms over my chest and glare at him. "You can't unilaterally decide to give me the money to buy Basil's business."

"It's my money and I'll do with it what I want."

Spoiler alert. Basil was right when he said Mercury's loaded. I don't know how much money he has, but when I asked to borrow fifty-thousand dollars he responded by telling me he'd have the cash for me in the morning. *The cash. In the morning.*

After I got my heart started again, I told him I didn't need cash. We've been arguing about the money every second since then.

"Why would you want to give it to me? You barely know me."

He narrows his eyes on me. "I know you, Mercy Keller."

He begins climbing the stairs again. I hurry to help him before he falls.

"Are you doing this because you want me to stay in Winter Falls?" I ask the question I've been wondering ever since he offered me the money.

"You belong here," he mutters as I open the door and usher him inside. "Now, get me some popcorn."

"Popcorn? This is a meeting. Not a movie theater."

He points to the back of the room where there's a popcorn stand set up.

"This is Winter Falls," he says as I help him into a seat.

I buy a bucket of popcorn and a couple of cokes, although most people are buying beer. The room is crowded and the atmosphere is festive. This isn't similar to any business meeting I've been to before. Although, I haven't been to many.

"We're here," Indigo says as she sits next to me. She isn't alone. Virginia and Leia are with her. She leans around me to wave at Mercury. "Hi, Uncle Mercury."

He grunts at her.

"What are you doing here?" I ask them.

"Duh." Indigo rolls her eyes. "Supporting you. It's what friends do."

"But how did you know about the meeting?"

"My boss told me," Leia says. "Which begs the question, why didn't you tell us?"

"Everything happened really fast. Basil offered to sell me the business two days ago and now I'm here."

"You should have messaged me," Leia says. "I majored in business. I could have helped with your presentation."

I gulp. I nearly forgot about the presentation.

Virginia scowls. "Way to scare her."

Indigo pats my arm. "You'll be fine. The town is excited about having new blood."

"Not everyone," Virginia mutters. "Especially not librarians who refuse to leave you alone even when they've 'retired'."

"If you kids won't quiet down, you need to move," Mercury grumbles.

"The meeting hasn't started yet."

He indicates the front of the room where a woman is standing holding a gable. She pounds it on the table. *Bang! Bang! Bang!*

"It is now," Mercury says.

"I now call the Winter Falls October Business Meeting to order."

"Who's she?" I whisper to Indigo.

"Rain. She's the mayor and the local jewelry store owner."

"Our first order of business," Rain says once everyone settles down and is quiet. "Is Basil's tow truck company. Mercy Keller has offered to buy the business."

"I approve!"

What the hell? Was that Gibson? I search the room and there he is. Standing in the back with the rest of the band.

"We haven't gotten to the voting portion of the evening," Rain says.

Gibson shrugs. "Doesn't matter. I vote Mercy can have Basil's business."

I ignore the butterflies exploding in my stomach at his vote of confidence. It's fake. He's fulfilling our agreement to act as my boyfriend in public. Nothing more.

"But she hasn't given her presentation yet. We need to make sure she has sufficient funds to take over the business and run it," Rain insists.

"I'll give her the money."

Oh no, he didn't. I'm not some helpless woman who needs her boyfriend to support her. I don't care if he's a rockstar and probably has enough money he can use the bills to wipe his ass. I'm my own independent woman.

I jump to my feet. "I don't need your money."

"I'm glad we bought popcorn for this," Indigo whispers, and I glare down at her.

She smiles. "What?"

"I'll deal with you later," I mutter. "One crazy person at a time."

"I'd take his money," Sage hollers.

"Me too. Yes, sirree bob. And if he wants a lap dance for his troubles, I'm in."

My mouth drops open at Feather's declaration. She smiles and mouths *he's hot* at me.

I know he's hot. I wouldn't have slept with him otherwise. But I don't run around sleeping with every man I find attractive. There needs to be a connection as well.

And with Gibson, there is a connection. Every time I look at him, my body warms and tingles spread through me. In anticipation of another kiss. Another round of sex.

I clear my throat. I can't believe I'm thinking about sex at the most important business meeting of my life. I must be sleep deprived. Or exhausted from two days of arguing with Uncle Mercury. Maybe my mind is on the fritz from all of the abrupt changes in my life.

"I wouldn't strip for him. My Orion has a fit when I'm naked in front of other men." Petal grins. "But he doesn't have a problem if men strip for me. What do you say, Gibson?"

Feather claps. "He can strip for sexy book club."

Gibson's gaze meets mine. "The only person I'm stripping for is Mercy."

Petal claps. "I knew this would be my favorite project."

I growl. "My life is not a project."

Bang! Bang! Bang!

Uncle Mercury pounds his cane on the floor before standing. "Mercy has the money and I vouch for her."

I steady him with a hand on his elbow. "I've prepared a presentation."

"What are you going to name the business?" Rain asks.

"*Wheely Great.*"

"Great play on words. I approve," Virginia says.

"Bring it to a vote," Mercury orders and I help him to sit.

"B-b-but," I sputter.

Indigo elbows me. "Shush. You won't have to give the presentation if they vote now."

"But what if the vote isn't in my favor?"

Leia rolls her eyes. "It'll be in your favor."

"How do you know?"

"I have my ways," she sings.

"All in favor?" Rain asks and I hold my breath as I wait for hands to be raised.

I scan the room. Almost every hand is in the air. The gossip gals have their hands raised. All the members of *Cash & the Sinners* have their hands raised. Uncle Mercury has his cane in the air.

Phew. I blow out a breath. I didn't expect the people of Winter Falls to support me.

Bang! "The motion carries." Rain smiles at me. "Welcome to Winter Falls, *Wheely Great.*"

"Happy to be here." I stand. "Thank you for your support. I won't forget it."

"And we won't let you forget it when we need a tow," someone shouts.

"*Wheely Great* is happy for your custom."

I collapse into my seat. I can't believe it. I did it. I bought a business. After what happened with Zeke, I thought it would take years for me to build another business. And, yet, here I am. Winter Falls rocks.

Don't ask me what happens for the rest of the meeting. I'm too filled with excitement and nervous energy to pay attention.

As soon as Rain announces the meeting is adjourned, I spring to my feet.

"I did it!" I squeal.

Indigo, Virginia, and Leia rush me for hugs.

"I'm excited you're staying in town," Virginia says.

"I never thought a small town in Colorado would be my home but here I am."

Uncle Mercury grunts from behind me. "Ain't nothing wrong with a small town."

"I didn't say there was. Here." I offer him my arm. "Let's get you home."

He bats away my arm. "You stay with your friends. I'll be fine."

I frown. How is he getting home without me? He shouldn't be driving a golf cart.

Gibson joins our group. "Mercy. Can we talk?"

I sigh. He wants to talk now? He couldn't have – I don't know – talked to me before he snuck out of the bed we shared? I haven't heard a word from him since.

"I'm taking my uncle home."

"I've got him," Virginia says. "I'm used to dealing with stubborn old people."

"Who you calling stubborn?" Mercury asks.

Dylan steps forward. "Watch your mouth when you speak to my Ginny."

Mercury studies Dylan. "I approve. You may escort me home now."

Dylan chuckles as he and Virginia help Mercury toward the exit.

"I won't wait up for you," Mercury shouts before leaving.

"We should get back to Isla," Leia says and Fender grunts in agreement before they leave.

Cash tugs on Indigo's wrist. "Come on. Time to go."

Indigo frowns. "Why? I want to watch Mercy give Gibson an earful. What was he thinking? Offering her money. He's supposed to be the charming one."

Sorry Cash mouths at me before dragging Indigo away.

"But I was having fun," she whines.

"I'll make it up to you."

I giggle at their antics. Having girlfriends is fun. Who knew?

"Mercy, can we talk?"

I glance around and realize Gibson and I are now alone in the room. Well, shit.

Chapter 19

Trust – an essential ingredient in a real relationship

GIBSON

I hold my breath as I wait for Mercy's response. I wouldn't blame her if she walked away. Not after I ran away from the bed we were sharing. And, apparently, offering to bank roll her business was a mistake as well. Not sure why.

She blows out a breath. "Fine. Let's do this."

"Maybe we should go somewhere private."

She throws out her arms and whirls around. "Pretty sure everyone in Winter Falls abandoned me here with you."

"No, they didn't." I point to the door where Sage and Feather are peeking through the window watching us.

"This town is full of busybodies."

"We prefer the term gossip gals," Sage hollers.

"Yeah," Feather adds. "We even have matching t-shirts. They're hot pink."

"Why did I decide to stay in Winter Falls again?" Mercy mutters.

I reach for her hand. "I'm glad you're staying."

She bats me away. "Why? So you can run away from me again? Or maybe you want to throw money at me again?"

"He can throw money at me any time," Sage shouts.

A muscle ticks in Mercy's jaw. She's about to explode.

I grasp her hand. "Let's go somewhere else."

I wait for her to push me away again. To my relief, she doesn't.

"Fine," she grits out.

I lead her out of the room.

"You're no fun, Gibson Lewis," Sage complains when we pass her.

"What's wrong?" Mercy taunts. "Can't find any fun on your own?"

I hurry her out of the building before the gossip gals can answer her. We reach Main Street and I glance around. Where can we go in town where we won't be overheard? There are people strolling up and down the street and when the door to the brewery opens, noise pours out.

There's no other choice. My house it is.

"Where are we going?" Mercy asks when we turn away from Main Street where almost all the businesses in Winter Falls are located.

"My place."

Her hand jerks in my hold. "Your place? I hope you don't think we're having a repeat of the other night."

My cock twitches at the idea of having Mercy back in my bed. I usually don't enjoy repeats with women I sleep with, but

Mercy is the exception. I'm starting to think she's the exception to every single rule I've ever written.

"We're talking. Just talking," I clarify.

"Fine," she grumbles.

"Good evening," Forest greets as we pass him.

Mercy stumbles and I rush to steady her before she lands face first on the sidewalk. "Are you okay?"

"I might be having hallucinations."

"Hallucinations?" I narrow my eyes on her. "You aren't on some type of hallucinogens, are you? Mushrooms are bad for you."

"How do you know?"

"Ask me some time about Jett's reaction to ingesting mushrooms. Long story short. Jett is no longer allowed to use hallucinogens and the driver on the tour bus now puts a paddle lock on his door."

She giggles. "You guys do have some crazy stories." She points behind her. "But I thought I was having hallucinations because I saw some guy walking squirrels."

"I believe they're chipmunks, not squirrels."

Her eyes widen. "I wasn't seeing things?"

"You're lucky he was wearing pants tonight."

Her mouth gapes open. "Does he not usually wear pants?"

"He says pants restrict his balls."

Her nose wrinkles. "You know. I can kind of understand where he's coming from. I hate wearing bras."

My gaze dips to her chest. Unfortunately, she is wearing a bra now. I wouldn't mind seeing her naked breasts again, those pretty pink nipples. I could suck on them until she goes crazy. My jeans tighten and my cock pushes against my zipper.

I inhale a deep breath and force sexy thoughts of Mercy away. I am not seducing her to get what I want. But if I get what I want, I will definitely be seducing her in the future. As often as I'm able.

"Shall we continue walking before your brain explodes from visions of me not wearing a bra?" Mercy teases.

"You weren't supposed to notice."

She nods toward my crotch. "Hard not to."

I smirk. "Thanks."

She rolls her eyes. "Typical man. The world could fall down around you but as long as someone complements your dick, you're happy."

I step closer to her. "If I recall correctly, my cock made you very happy the other day."

She pushes me away. "And then you fled the bed because you're a big fat chicken."

"I had a moment of insanity."

She snorts. "A moment? It's been three days and not a peep from you until you announced in front of the whole town that you want to be my sugar daddy."

"He can be my sugar daddy anytime!" Clove waves from her front porch.

"Aren't you married?" Mercy hollers at Clove.

"We can be in one of those polyamorous relationships. We read a book about one in sexy book club."

"Sorry, I'm a one woman man," I declare.

Mercy bursts into laughter. "Good one."

"I'm not joking."

She waves away my words. "You kidder, you."

I'm not kidding. I'm no longer interested in other women. Only Mercy.

I shackle her wrist and haul her toward my rental house. I'm done with people interrupting me. It's hard enough trying to figure out what I need to say to Mercy without the entire town adding their two cents.

"Why did you offer to be my sugar daddy?" Mercy asks once we're behind closed doors.

"I'm your boyfriend. I'm supposed to be supportive."

"You're my *fake* boyfriend."

"I don't want to be your fake boyfriend anymore."

She sighs. "I figured this was coming. Do you want to stage a public breakup or tell everyone we're done? And what reason are we going to give? The nosy Nellies in this town are going to want a reason."

I stalk toward her until her back is up against the wall. "We're not breaking up. We're making this real."

"What? Real? We agreed. This isn't real."

"Felt awful real to me the other night when I was buried deep inside you and you were shouting my name in ecstasy."

She glares at me. "I did not shout your name."

I smirk. "Yeah, you did."

Her nostrils flare as she inhales a deep breath. "Nevertheless. We agreed this would be fake."

"We also agreed we wouldn't have sex. Things change."

"I knew having sex with you was a mistake," she mutters.

"No." I slam my hands next to her head on the wall and lean in until I'm close enough to breathe in her spicy scent. "Me and you are not a mistake. Never a mistake."

She studies my face. "You're serious. You want this to be real."

"It *is* real."

"Why the change? You were dead set on not entering into a relationship before."

I scowl. I don't want to explain my boring past to her but I have to give her something if I'm going to convince her I want something real with her. "Let's just say, love hasn't treated me well before."

She snorts. "And it has me? My ex cheated on me and then stole the business I'd built up."

I cringe. "I'm sorry that happened to you."

"In lieu of sympathy, I'll accept an explanation."

"I walked right into that, didn't I?"

"I did leave the door wide open for you."

I grin. This woman is amazing. I'm having one of the most serious conversations of my life and she makes me smile. No wonder I'm falling for her. She's perfect for me.

I kiss her forehead before stepping back and starting to pace the room. "I'm trusting you here."

She crosses her arms over her chest and leans back against the wall. "If you don't think you can trust me, there's no chance we can build a relationship."

Damn. She's right. "I do trust you."

She raises her eyebrows.

"I do," I insist and I realize with a start my words are true. Mercy would never sell my story to the tabloids. Hell, she still doesn't know the extent of my fame because she prefers country music and refuses to google me. That's a problem for another day.

I blow out a breath. "But I've never told anyone about this before."

The fight bleeds out of her eyes. "If you're not ready to tell me, I'll understand."

"Don't do that."

"Do what?"

"Be perfect."

She smirks. "I can't help it. I was born this way."

I make my way across the room to her and frame her face with my hands. I kiss her nose before closing my eyes and blurting out, "My parents sued me for all my money after *Cash & the Sinners* got famous."

She gasps. "Are you kidding me?"

I open my eyes to find hers are filled with righteous anger. "I wish I were kidding you."

"Where do they live? Do they own cars? I'm a mechanic. I know how to cut brake lines and no one will ever figure it out."

"Are you offering to kill my parents?"

She places a finger over my lips. "Shush. I never said the word kill. You assumed it."

I kiss her finger. "Now you know why I don't do relationships."

"My mom's an alcoholic. I never met my dad. And I only met my uncle because Mom found out he's rich and sent me here to put him in a nursing home. And you know about my asshole ex cheating and stealing from me."

"What are you saying?"

She shrugs. "My life resembles a country music song."

"At least you realize how cliché country music is."

"Nope." She throws daggers out of her eyes at me. "It resembles life."

She places a hand on my cheek. "As does your story. It's shitty what happened to you but you can't let it stop you from living your life."

I place my forehead against hers. "That's exactly what I'm trying to do. I'm trying to live my life. *With you.* What do you say? You want to make this fake relationship into something real?"

She bites her lip. Those bright red lips are tempting. I have at least a thousand ideas of what I want to do with them, to them. But I stay my path. I'm not using sex to convince her.

"I need to think about it."

I frown and she taps my nose. "I'm not saying no. I'm saying my life is moving faster than Uncle Mercury's Dodge Charger and I need a moment to catch up."

I kiss her forehead before stepping away. "I understand."

"You do?"

I do. Am I happy she didn't jump at the chance to date me? Hell no. But I can understand her needing time. I spent two days contemplating what to do after I realized I'm falling for her. I can give her the same courtesy.

Chapter 20

Pretending – only works when people don't know you're faking

MERCY

> **Good morning, sassy girl**

I frown at the message from Gibson. He sends them constantly. Sweet little messages to remind me he's thinking of me. Or, they would be sweet, if he wasn't pushing me. Apparently agreeing to give me time doesn't mean not pushing me. Sneaky man.

> **How did you sleep?**

> **Are you having a good day?**

I groan. Why does he have to be sweet? No one's ever asked me about my day before. Not even my mom when I was little.

"Hey, Mercy!" Indigo shouts.

My brow wrinkles as I walk out of the garage to discover Indigo standing with Virginia and Leia in the driveway.

"What are you doing here?"

"We're here to convince you to stay with Gibson," Leia says.

Indigo slaps her shoulder. "You weren't supposed to tell her."

Virginia snorts. "Because this is a secret mission?"

Indigo crosses her arms over her chest. "This *is* a secret mission."

"You've been hanging around the gossip gals too much," Leia grumbles.

"And you're starting to resemble your grumpy man."

Leia waves her hand in the air. "I think you mean grumpy fiancé."

"Oh my god!" I squeal and rush to hug her. "Congratulations."

"What happened? Did he get down on one knee? Or just grunt at you?" I ask when we pull apart.

Indigo pushes her way in between us. "We'll tell you all about it when you come with us."

I motion to the garage. "I'm still at work."

"And you're the boss now so you can leave whenever you want."

I frown. "I'm not the boss yet."

"Go on. Get out of here," Basil hollers from under the hood of the car we're currently restoring. "You're not going to get anymore work done today now anyway."

"Thanks, boss."

"Not your boss anymore," he mutters.

Technically, he's still my boss until we finish the paperwork but he's obviously ready to retire.

"Let's go." Indigo tries to herd me away, but I plant my feet.

"I'm not going anywhere in this attire." I motion to my overalls, which are covered in grease and paint. "And I need to get home to Uncle Mercury anyway."

"Mercury's handled," Virginia says. "Gratitude is going to sit with him."

"Gratitude?" My brow wrinkles. "Your former boss?"

She shrugs. "Apparently, they're friends."

Indigo shoos me toward the restroom. "Now get out of the overalls and get ready to go."

I debate fighting them some more but I could use a night out with my friends. Spending another night pacing around my bedroom trying to figure out what to do about Gibson isn't appealing. Plus, Mercury threatened to shoot me with birdshot if I didn't settle down. Yep. A night out is what's needed.

"Where are we going?" I ask once we're settled in a golfcart driving away from the garage.

Virginia sighs. "My house."

My brow wrinkles. "If you don't want us in your house, we can go somewhere else. Not my place. Obviously. I don't actually have a place. But somewhere else."

"No, can do," Indigo announces. "Cash and the gang are at my house doing whatever it is musicians do when they get together."

I scowl. I hope Gibson isn't drinking. If he drinks, I am done with him. I don't date men who can't stick to the agreements they make.

Although, we agreed he wouldn't drink while we're *fake* dating. What happens if our relationship isn't fake anymore? Something to consider.

"And my daughter Isla is at my house with her babysitter," Leia says.

I pat Virginia's arm. "Sorry about invading your place."

"She doesn't care," Indigo claims.

Judging by Virginia's pursed lips she does care but those two have been friends since high school. I'm not getting in between them.

We arrive at Virginia's house which is a few doors down from Indigo's and hop out of the golf cart. I feel my phone vibrate in my pocket and pull it out.

Have fun with your girls tonight.

How does he know what I'm doing? Is he spying on me? I look up to scan the area and nearly bang my head against Leia's.

"Are you reading my texts?"

"Don't worry. He's not spying on you. Indigo told Cash we're getting together tonight."

I guess she was reading my text.

"Come on." She laces her arm through mine. "Time to get the inquisition over,"

"Inquisition?"

She tugs me forward. "It's fine. They won't actually torture you."

Crap. In the excitement about her engagement, I totally forgot their mission was to convince me to stay with Gibson. I drag my feet but Leia's strong for being tiny. She hauls me into the house and pushes me onto the sofa.

Virginia walks in carrying a tray with champagne glasses. She tries to hand me one but I shake my head.

"I don't drink, remember? Not even on special occasions."

"It's sparkling grape juice."

"Who's pregnant?"

She sighs. "No one's pregnant, silly. I got the grape juice for you. You don't drink, so we don't drink."

I snatch a glass from the tray. "Thanks, but you can drink in front of me. I don't mind."

"Except you do mind when it's Gibson who drinks," Indigo says.

Leia chuckles. "Way to be subtle."

"Oh, please. This one is wily. We can't be subtle with her if we want to get our way."

I lift my glass. "To Leia and Fender. May they live happily ever after."

"Told you she's wily," Indigo mumbles as we clink glasses.

I finish my grape juice, which is just as disgusting as it's always been, and set my glass on the coffee table. I motion to Indigo. "Out with it."

She doesn't hesitate. "You should give Gibson a chance."

"Give Gibson a chance?" I furrow my brow. "I've given him a chance. We've been dating for a while now."

Leia snorts. "You don't honestly think anyone believes this fake dating stuff, do you?"

My pulse races. They know it's fake. Shit. Who else knows? Does Uncle Mercury? No wonder he can't pick a nursing home to move into.

No. I refuse to believe it. Gibson and I played the part well. They can't possibly know it was all fake.

"What do you mean fake?"

"I figured it out when we told you a naked woman had come on to Gibson after one of the concerts," Virginia says. "You had no idea what we were talking about."

"Ha!" Indigo shouts. "I figured it out before you. At the brewery to be precise. The way he kissed you it was obvious it was the first kiss. If you had really been dating Gibson, there's no way he could have kept his lips off yours for very long."

I touch my lips with my hand. "What's wrong with my lips?"

She snorts. "Are you kidding? I'm straight *and* in love with Cash and I still want to kiss you to find out how those plump, red lips feel."

I feel my cheeks warm but I ignore it. "Sorry. I don't do women. Been there. Done that. Didn't get off."

"I knew before all of you," Leia declares. "When we met you at the party and you didn't bat an eyelash after I explained about the bet between Gibson and Jett, I knew. No way would you have dated Gibson any longer if you knew he and Jett were betting about who could bed the most women."

Crap on a stale cracker. I totally forgot about the bet. How the hell could I possibly forget the man I'm considering dating is a complete and total man whore?

"Leia!" Indigo shouts. "You're scaring her. She's never going to give Gibson a chance now."

I narrow my eyes on her. "Maybe Gibson doesn't want a chance. This is fake after all. According to you three, at least."

"Oh, it's fake all right. It also stopped being fake when the two of you had sex the other day."

I gasp. "How do you know we had sex?"

"A woman knows," Indigo sings.

Leia elbows her. "Gibson's house is next to mine. I saw you leave the next morning with sex hair."

"And you had to tell her?" I point at Indigo.

She shrugs. "Apparently, it's a sisterhood and there are no secrets."

Indigo leans forward. "You had sex so why don't you want to give Gibson a chance at something real?"

I debate jumping to my feet and running out of the house. I don't owe them any explanations.

Virginia places her hand on my thigh. "You don't have to tell her anything."

"Yes, she does. She's our new best friend. Besties share everything," Indigo claims.

Virginia squeezes my thigh. "I can escort you out the back door while Leia holds Indigo off." Leia nods to indicate her agreement with the plan. "But," she continues. "We are your friends and we're here for you if you want to discuss anything. I wasn't exactly jumping for joy at the chance to love a rockstar."

"Same." Leia nods. "I didn't want to fall for a rockstar either."

Indigo crosses her arms over her chest. "I didn't fall in love with a rockstar. I fell in love with Cash who became a rockstar."

"Here's the thing," Leia begins. "Gibson is different with you."

"Different how?"

"Before you, Gibson didn't have girlfriends." Her cheeks darken. "He had conquests. He didn't know their names. Didn't care about them. He mostly asked Fender to kick them out while he hid in the bathroom."

"Man whore," I mutter.

"But with you he's different. Before you, he would have jumped on the naked woman in the shower."

My stomach sours at the idea of a woman throwing herself at my man.

"But he didn't," Leia reminds me. "Because of you."

"And he isn't drinking," Virginia adds.

"Because I made him stop."

Virginia shakes her head. "Honey, you know better than anyone here you can't make a person stop drinking."

I have to admit it. They make some good points.

"I have a super bad record with men."

"Who doesn't?" Leia asks. "Isla's father left when she was a baby."

"It's okay to be scared," Indigo says. "We've all been there. Love is scary."

I realize she's right. I am scared. Why am I scared? I've never been scared to start a relationship before.

Because those men didn't mean to me what Gibson does. Shit on a stick shift. I'm falling for Gibson.

Chapter 21

GIBSON

It's been five days since I've seen Mercy. I'm officially done waiting for her to come to me. And, damn it, I've missed her. I've missed her laugh. I've missed her sass. I've missed her. Period. Messaging on the phone is not the same.

I'm beginning to understand why Cash, Fender, and Dylan get antsy when we're gone from Winter Falls too long. If I'm lucky, I'll be annoyingly antsy on our next mini-tour.

I park in the driveway in front of Mercy's garage and scan the area. Basil's house is next door but otherwise the garage sits on land in the middle of a field far away from the rest of Winter Falls.

I climb out of the car and walk to the side entrance of the garage. I knock but when no one answers I try the door. It's unlocked.

I enter the garage and realize why no one answered my knock. The radio is blaring music. I have no problem with blaring music but country? Really? I'm going to convert my sassy girl to a rock listener if it's the last thing I do.

I find the radio and switch to a rock station. I smile when I realize the *Cash & the Sinners* song *Resurrect* is playing.

"Basil, switch the music back!" Mercy hollers from underneath the car she's working on.

"Wasn't me!" He yells from where he's working on some engine part on a table in the corner. He glances over at me and winks. I lift my chin in greeting.

Mercy glides out from underneath the car. I wait near the radio for her. She gets to her feet and scowls at me.

I ignore the scowl since I'm too busy being enchanted by her body. She's wearing overalls but the top is pulled down and tied around her waist exposing her sports bra and the smooth skin of her stomach. As she stomps toward me, her breasts bounce and my mouth waters.

My cock twitches. He wants to fuck those breasts. I fist my hands before I reach for her and draw her into my arms. I still need to convince her to be mine. To give us a chance.

"Lead mechanic chooses the music," she declares as she reaches for the radio.

I snatch her wrist to stop her. "Just listen to this song."

Her eyes narrow. "Is it one of yours?"

I nod. "Cash wrote it for Indigo when he was trying to win her back."

She grins. "Ah, how sweet."

I used to think it was disgusting. Why write a song for one woman? There are plenty of them to choose from. You don't need to get stuck on one of them.

But then I met Mercy and I'm starting to get it. I'm starting to get all of it. Why men give up careers for women. Why men choose to forgo other women for *the one.*

"This song isn't bad," she says after the chorus finishes.

I chuckle. "Isn't bad? It's been at the top of the charts for months now."

Her eyes widen. "Really?"

I tweak her nose. "Really. Have you not googled the band yet?"

"Nope. And I don't plan to either."

I used to get annoyed about how she didn't care about the band. Not anymore. I'm enjoying how she likes me – Gibson Lewis – for who I am. Because I am more than a rockstar. I am more than a man who can play the guitar. And fame eventually fades.

The song ends and I lower the volume.

"I'll convert you to rock music eventually."

She rolls her eyes. "In your dreams, guitar man. In your dreams."

"At least you realize I play the guitar."

Her eyes twinkle. "Well, you definitely don't sing."

I lower my voice. "What's wrong with my voice?" Her eyes flare and I step closer. "You don't enjoy the sound of my voice? You don't enjoy it when I whisper naughty words into your ear while I'm buried deep inside you?" Her breath hitches and I reach for her.

"Ahem!" Basil clears his voice as he slides past us. "I'm taking a break for lunch." He winks at me. "A long lunch."

"Now, where were we?" I ask once the door shuts behind him.

Mercy shuffles away from me. "I was wondering what you're doing here since you agreed to give me space until I make a decision about us."

Damn. No sexy times on top of the hood of the car Mercy's working on. My cock protests.

"I have a surprise for you." And I missed you.

She motions to my crotch. "I hope that's not my surprise."

I smirk. "It's a bonus."

She blows out a breath. "I'm serious, Gibson. What are you doing here?"

"And I'm serious. I have a surprise."

"A real surprise? Not the one-eyed snake in your pants?"

I chuckle. "A real surprise."

"Where is it?"

I hold out my hand. "Let me show you."

Relief fills my chest when she doesn't hesitate to take my hand. The second we touch, sparks fly from her skin to mine. Yep. This woman is meant for me.

I lead her out of the garage to the driveway where her surprise is parked.

She gasps and tugs out of my hold to run to the car. "Is this a 1965 Ford Mustang Shelby GT350?"

She doesn't wait for my answer before continuing. "Where did you get it? There were less than six-hundred of these built. How did you find it? Did you buy it? Does she drive?"

I dangle the keys in front of her face. "I drove it over here."

She snatches the keys from me and rushes to the driver's door. When I don't move, she motions to the passenger seat. "Get in. This is the surprise, right? I get to drive an original Shelby?"

I shove my hands in my pockets. "Um, actually…"

Her eyes narrow. "You better not have bought this car for me."

"I didn't." I wouldn't dare buy her a car worth half a million dollars. She'd skin me alive before decapitating me and marching around town with my head on a stick.

"Is this car yours?"

"It is."

"How long have you owned it?"

My sassy girl is too smart for her own good. "Two days." Because it took the seller two days to get the car to Colorado.

She studies the car. "It needs restoration."

"Lucky for me, I happen to know a mechanic who restores classic cars."

She crosses her arms over her chest and glares at me. "You don't have to buy me business."

"I'm not. I need a car if I'm going to stay in Winter Falls."

"You're staying in Winter Falls?"

I shrug. "I don't have anywhere else to go and I like it here." I like one person in particular.

"Even if you can't buy beer here?"

I nod. "Even if."

"Even if you have to stay sober?"

"Not buying beer kind of implies staying sober."

"I'm not joking, Gibson. I don't know if I can be with a man who drinks."

I rush to her. "Are you saying what I think you're saying?"

She blows out a breath and stares off in the distance. "I have a bad record with men and relationships."

I grasp her hands. "And I have no record with women and relationships. Together we'll figure it out."

"You're sure?" The insecurity in her eyes nearly brings me to my knees. My sassy girl should never be insecure.

I pull her close and wrap my arms around her. "I wouldn't ask you to take a chance on me if I wasn't sure."

"Okay," she whispers.

My head lowers, my mouth intent on meeting hers, on tasting her again. But she places a hand in front of her mouth to stop me.

"But no sex."

I'm confused. "No sex?"

She nods. "No sex. I've always jumped into the physical part of a relationship and then regretted it later when it turned out the guy I'm 'seeing' is a complete meathead who thinks women should cater to his every whim."

"I don't want you to cater to my every whim. And I'm not a meathead."

She raises her eyebrows. "You aren't? You didn't offer to bankroll my business in front of the entire town?"

"I was desperate for your attention."

"Desperate?"

"I hadn't seen you for days."

"And whose fault was that?"

"Mine. I'm the idiot here."

"It's good you recognize your faults."

I chuckle. "And I suppose you don't have any?"

"Well, it is kind of annoying how often I'm right."

I kiss her nose. "I love your modesty."

"Being awesome is a heavy burden."

"Okay. No sex."

Her shoulders relax. "Thank you."

I frown. Did she think I'd push her for sex? Does she not know me better by now? Maybe it is better we refrain from the physical part until we know each other better.

Those are words I never thought I'd ever think. I'm enjoying a lot of firsts with Mercy.

"I won't push you for sex," I growl.

"It's not you. It's me. You might say I don't have much impulse control when it comes to you."

I grin. "When it comes to me? You can't resist me."

She rolls her eyes and pushes me away. "Do you want to go for a ride in the Shelby or is your ego too big to fit inside?"

I walk to the passenger door. "We might as well go for a ride since other rides are now off the table." We settle in the car. "Speaking of which, how long are other rides off the table?"

She shrugs. "I don't know. I'll let you know when I know."

Is it possible to get instantaneous blue balls? If so, I have them. Mercy is going to test my control, but she's worth it. I know she is.

"What about first base? Second base?" I waggle my eyebrows. "Third base?"

"Oh my god. How old are you again?"

"I'm thirty. Do you want to card me?"

"Kissing is okay. But no touching," she orders as she switches on the car. Her eyes light with excitement as she revs the engine.

"I no longer care why you bought this car," she says as she switches to first gear and we shoot out of the driveway.

I quickly don my seatbelt and settle in for the ride. I'm not an adrenaline junkie the way Jett is but I do enjoy speed.

But what I enjoy most of all is watching how happy Mercy is as she drives the muscle car. Her smile stretches from ear to ear and her eyes sparkle with excitement.

"Hold on tight!" She shouts.

Oh, baby, I am holding on tight. I'm going to hold on tight to you until you fall for me the way I've fallen for you.

Chapter 22

Busted – when you realize you weren't fooling anyone

MERCY

I pull the curtain in the living room aside as I watch for Gibson to arrive. We're going out on a date tonight. A real date. No more fake.

And I'm freaking out. What do you do on a date when sex and booze is off the table? Can we talk to each other for hours and not get bored?

Will Gibson still want me when I'm no longer a challenge?

A Hummer pulls into the driveway and stops in front of the porch. I rush to the front door. "Bye, Uncle Mercury. I'll be back in a few hours."

Don't worry. I'm not actually leaving my uncle alone. Gratitude is coming over again in a little while.

"Have your young man come in the house since he's now your boyfriend," Mercury orders.

I freeze with my hand on the door handle. "What do you mean *now*? Gibson's been my boyfriend for a while."

He snorts. "You don't seriously think you can fool me, do you?" Actually, I did.

I sigh before I spin around to face him. "What gave it away?"

He chuckles. "I'm not giving up my secrets."

I narrow my eyes on him. "Who told you? Does the whole town know?"

He shrugs. I recognize the tactic. It's easier to maintain a lie if you don't actually speak.

I perch on the coffee table in front of him. "Does this mean you're not moving into a nursing home?"

He scowls. "Ain't no reason for me to move into a nursing home. You're here now, aren't you?"

I frown. "Did you loan me the money to buy Basil's business so I wouldn't leave?"

"Not a loan."

I wave away his words. It is a loan. He just doesn't realize it yet. "Answer the question."

"I don't have anyone else to give the money to anyway."

"Uncle Mercury," I begin. "I'm not running away. I'm staying in Winter Falls. But I can't care for you all the time. I have a business to run now." And Gibson.

"There's nothing for you to worry about."

"The doctor said—"

"I'm not talking about the quack." He pulls a sheet of paper from behind his back and hands it to me.

"What's this?"

"A schedule."

I study the paper. It is a schedule. A schedule for the next two weeks of who is looking after Mercury at what time. My mouth gapes open.

"You're letting the people of Winter Falls help you?"

"You're staying in Winter Falls?"

"I kind of like it here." I narrow my eyes on him. "Grumpy old men not withstanding."

He snatches the paper back from me. "Do we have an agreement?"

"What are your terms?"

"You agree not to put me in a nursing home and you continue to live here in this house with me."

"And you'll agree to have someone to sit with you whenever I can't be home?" He nods. "And you won't growl and grumble at them until they leave?"

He scowls. "That happened one time."

"Clove's still mad at you for saying her coffee wasn't as good as yours."

He grunts. "She's married to Sirius. She should be used to grumpy men by now."

He's not wrong. I hold out my hand. "Deal?"

He shakes my hand. "And I'm leaving this house and my money to you when I die."

"First of all, you're a crotchety old man. You're never dying. Secondly, I don't want your house or your money."

"It's yours anyway." He points to the door with his cane. "Your young man is here."

I kiss his forehead. "Don't wait up for me."

"Use protection!" He shouts after me.

I'm sure my face is bright red when I open the door. "Ignore him. Everyone else does."

"Don't ignore me! You don't want no baby yet."

I hang my head, but Gibson chuckles.

"I think I like your uncle."

"Then, you don't know him very well," I mutter.

"I heard you."

"I know," I holler at Uncle Mercury. "You have the hearing of a bat."

Gibson grasps my hand. "You ready to go or do you want to shout at your uncle some more before we leave?"

I pretend to consider the matter. "I'm good."

"Bye, Mr. Mercury," Gibson calls.

I hurry him out the door before Uncle Mercury starts a lecture about the use of Mr. and why it's ruining society. I've heard it once already. And I still don't know what he was going on about.

I screech to a halt when I realize the Hummer has an electric motor. "No."

Gibson's brow wrinkles. "No, what?"

"I'm not going anywhere in that, that thing masquerading as a vehicle."

"Too big for you?" He waggles his eyebrows and I slap his stomach.

"It's not about size." Not *all* about size. "Where's the roar of the engine? The vibration of the engine? And all electric vehicles are automatic." I shiver. "Where's the fun in driving a car without shifting?"

He chuckles. "I knew you were a mechanic. I didn't realize you're a gearhead."

I roll my eyes. "Of course, I'm a gearhead." I lift my hands in the air. "Do you realize how long I have to wash my hands to get the grease out from underneath my nails?"

I don't wait for him to answer and tug him toward the garage. "We'll take the Charger."

"Your uncle won't mind?"

I shrug. "Since he just declared he's leaving me his house and fortune when he dies, I think not."

He pauses. "What?"

"Don't worry. I told him no."

"Why? He's your uncle. You're caring for him. You deserve it."

My eyes widen. "I deserve it? I'm not caring for my uncle because I want his money. I'm not my mother. I'm caring for him because he's my uncle and he needs it. I only wish I'd known about him years ago. I would have never let him live all alone if I had."

"You're a good person, Mercy Keller."

I snort. "You're the first person to think I am."

He wraps his arms around me and squeezes me tight. "You're a good person, Mercy."

To my shock, my eyes itch with unshed tears. What is happening? I don't cry because a man says I'm a good person. Unless the man is the one I'm falling for and he has his arms wrapped around me. Apparently, then, I do. I sniff and force the tears away.

"Where are we going?" I ask as he releases me.

He kisses my nose. "It's a surprise."

"I'll need directions since you aren't driving Uncle Mercury's car."

"Why not? Don't trust me?"

"I trust you. But not with this baby." Or with my heart. Yet.

We settle in the car and I switch on the engine. Gibson chuckles.

"What?"

"The excitement on your face when you're about to drive this car is a thing of beauty."

I roll my eyes. "You can flatter me all you want. I'm not having sex with you yet."

He places his hand on top of mine on the gearbox. "I know, sassy girl. I know. And I respect your decision."

"You respect my decision or you're afraid of what I'll do if you push me?"

He raises his palms in the air. "Why can't it be both?"

He gives me directions as I drive. The radio station plays country music and Gibson even hums along a few times. I smile. I'll convert him to a country music fan eventually.

"Turn left here," he says once we reach the outskirts of White Bridge.

"This is an alley."

"Thanks for stating the obvious."

I drive through the alley until we reach a door. "You can stop and park here."

"We'll block the alley if we stop here."

"It's a private driveway."

"Okay," I say as I switch off the engine. "Where are we? Is this the part where you skin me alive and sell my organs to the highest bidder?"

"Do I skin you alive before or after I sell off your organs?"

"Huh. Good question. Maybe you're only selling off my organs."

The door opens and a man in a suit with a clipboard steps outside. He nods to Gibson who waves in return.

"Is this the guy who's going to remove the organs?"

"You're crazy," he mutters. "Or are you scared?"

"Please. Scared isn't part of my vocabulary."

"Then, get out of the car and find out where we are." Gibson doesn't wait for me before opening his door. I rush to follow him. I'm not scared but I am curious.

"Mr. Lewis," clipboard man greets Gibson. "Thank you for arriving on time."

"You can thank me. I drove," I say and extend my hand. "I'm Mercy."

He purses his lips before nodding at me. I let my hand drop. Guess clipboard dude doesn't shake hands.

"This way please." He doesn't wait for a reply before whirling around and marching away.

Gibson grasps my hand and we follow him.

"Is this some reenactment of Frankenstein?" I whisper.

"Not very patient, are you?"

I shrug. "Never promised I was."

"Are you ready?" Clipboard dude asks when we stop.

The area is barely lit but I'm guessing by the echo we're in a large room.

"Ready," Gibson says.

The lights flicker on and I gasp at the sight in front of me. We're standing in a garage filled with luxury cars. And none of those sissy electric ones either.

"Where are we?"

"It's a private collection," Clipboard dude explains. "I ask you to respect the vehicles. The doors are unlocked." He checks his watch. "You have thirty minutes."

He starts to walk away, but I stop him. "Do you have a creeper?"

"Pardon me. What is a creeper?"

"A board on wheels used by mechanics to get under the car," I explain.

"I will procure one for you," he says as he walks away.

As soon as he's gone, I squeal and throw myself at Gibson. "Thank you. This is awesome. How did you arrange it?"

He wraps his arms around me but I push out of his hold. "No time for cuddling now. I have cars to examine."

"Don't I get a kiss in thank you?"

I push on my toes and kiss his cheek. "Thank you, Gibson. Best surprise ever."

You're making me fall in love with you. I force thoughts of love out of my mind. Now is not the time to contemplate how he's going to break my heart. Nope. I have cars to admire.

Chapter 23

Boob – as good a place as any to get an autograph

GIBSON

"Where the hell is Jett?" Cash growls at me.

"Why are you asking me?"

Dylan rolls his eyes. "Are you seriously asking? Maybe because you're Tweedle Dee and he's Tweedle Dum?"

I grit my teeth. "Stop calling me that name."

Fender snorts. "The same way you stopped calling me grumpapottamus when I asked."

I shrug. "If the name fits."

Fender growls and steps toward me but Dylan clears his throat and nods toward the press waiting on the other side of the studio. We're in the recording studio so they can't actually hear us but I wouldn't put it past them to make up what we're saying. It wouldn't be the first time.

"Has anyone heard from Jett?" Dylan asks the room but everyone's attention focuses on me.

"I haven't heard from him. I've been kind of busy."

"*Being busy* never stopped you and Jett from pulling your shenanigans before," Fender says.

I glare at him. "You better not be comparing Mercy to the fans and groupies."

The door opens and our manager, Mike, stomps in. "Where the hell is Jett? I can't keep the fans waiting much longer."

"We can start without him," I suggest.

"We can't start without Jett. The rest of *Cash & the Sinners* are in committed relationships," he spits out. "I need at least one of you to flirt with the fans."

The implication is obvious. I used to be the one who flirted with the fans at these meet and greets.

Cash clears his throat. "There's no actual requirement for us to flirt with fans during these events."

Mike glares at him. "Those fans out there didn't spend days phoning into radio stations to win a meet and greet with *Cash & the Sinners*."

"They didn't?" Fender growls.

"They want the fantasy of some rockstar falling in love with them. Which means you need to flirt with them."

"In my experience," I say. "I don't need to flirt for fans to think I can fall in love with them. In fact, they don't need any encouragement at all."

Mike sighs. "You had to throw the naked woman out of your shower? You couldn't kiss her at least?"

Mike's a good manager but I'm going to have his ass fired if he doesn't reel it in. I nearly lost Mercy once because of the antics of fans. I'm not risking losing her again. My sassy girl brought the sunshine back into my life. I'm not returning to the dark.

"I am not kissing fans to please you," I grit out.

Cash, Dylan, and Fender move to stand behind me.

"None of us are," Cash says.

"Love has ruined all of you," Mike mutters.

The door bangs open behind him.

"Love hasn't ruined me," Jett declares as he saunters into the room.

I rush to him. "Where have you been?"

I slap him on the back and he winces.

"Are you hurt? I told you the surfing competition wasn't a good idea."

He smirks. "It wasn't a good idea. It was an excellent idea."

I roll my eyes. "Did you finally find a woman to lower her standards for you?"

"Don't be jealous I'm winning."

I bite my tongue before I tell him I no longer give a shit about winning our bet. He can sleep with as many women as he wants. I'm only interested in sleeping with one woman. One very sassy woman who's my match in and out of bed.

"What the hell, Jett?" Cash asks. "We were worried about you."

"With good reason." Dylan waves toward Jett's head.

I step closer. There's a ragged scar about two inches long near his temple. "What the hell happened? And why didn't you contact us?"

He waggles his eyebrows. "I had company."

I cross my arms and glare at him. "You still should have contacted us."

"It was fine. One night in the hospital was all."

"You were in the hospital and didn't call? What the hell, Jett? I'm your emergency contact. I should have been informed."

"Like I said, I wasn't alone."

"What happened?" Dylan asks.

"I hit my head."

Dylan sighs. "I can see you hit your head. How did it happen?"

"I fell while surfing. I got a new scar and a concussion as a participation prize."

"Are you trying to break the record on how many concussions a person can get?" I ask.

"Nah. I don't play football."

"If you're done, can we start with the meet and greet?" Mike checks his watch. "Which is now officially thirty minutes off schedule."

"I thought Aurora was the one who had a hard-on for schedules," I joke.

Jett grimaces. I am so done with Jett and Aurora and their hate-on. They need to get over it already. We're professionals. They need to act as such.

Mike ushers us forward and we line up behind him. We walk through the sound room. "Ready?" He doesn't wait for an answer before opening the door.

Immediately the crowd starts to chant. *Sinners! Sinners! Sinners!*

Jett throws his hands in the air. "Who's ready to meet and greet me?"

Women rush to him and the security team hurries to protect him from being crushed.

"Shouldn't you take it easy after your concussion?" I have to shout to be heard.

A woman bats her eyelashes at him. "I can take care of you. I'm a nurse."

Jett waggles his eyebrows. "I always did enjoy playing doctor."

I guess he's fine. I leave him to do his thing.

"Gibson, Gibson!" A woman waves to get my attention.

"Hi," I greet.

"Can I get an autograph?"

"Sure." This is what we're here for today after all. Greeting fans who won the chance to meet the members of *Cash & the Sinners*.

She whips open her blouse to reveal her naked chest. "On the right boob. It's bigger."

Shit. Shit. Shit. What do I do? Mercy lost her mind about the naked woman in the shower and we were only fake dating then. Now we're the real deal, and I don't want to risk her wrath.

"I already have an appointment to have my tattoo guy ink over it."

She is not making things better.

I should have anticipated this. It's not my first meet and greet the fans day. And it's definitely not the first time a fan flashed her tits at me either. Not even close.

"What do I do?" I ask Dylan.

"Didn't you discuss this with Mercy before today?"

That would have been a good idea. Had I thought of it. But Mercy doesn't enjoy talking about me being a rockstar. Except when she teases me about never googling me. The woman seriously has no clue how big *Cash & the Sinners* is and she doesn't care.

Dylan chuckles. "Good luck, man."

I dig the marker out of my back pocket. I keep my eyes focused on the woman's shoulder as I sign her skin right below her collar bone.

"Thanks," she says as she buttons up her shirt.

Huh. Maybe this won't be as bad as I thought.

Two hours later I've come to a different conclusion. It is as bad as I thought.

"Come on, Gibson," the latest woman cajoles. "I promise I'll give you the time of your life."

I snort. As if some nameless, faceless woman can compete with Mercy.

"Not interested."

"He's boring now because he has a girlfriend," Jett hollers.

Naturally, the press hear. The paparazzi aren't allowed at our meet and greets but there's still press to make sure the day is documented on social media and in news stories. Let the questions commence.

"You have a girlfriend?"

"Who is she?"

"Does she live in Winter Falls?"

Crap. I don't want them knowing about Mercy and where she lives. Although, I don't have to worry about Mercy getting scared. She'd probably drive them out of town with her uncle's Charger while cackling the whole way.

Mike claps his hands to gain everyone's attention. "The band members will not be entertaining personal questions today."

My mouth gapes open at his announcement. Mike's never had a problem using our personal lives to gain press coverage before. Don't get me wrong. The guy's a good manager. But he's also a vulture who will do anything to ensure the band stays in the limelight.

"I spoke to him this morning," Cash mutters to me.

I cock an eyebrow in question.

"We don't need a repeat of what happened with Virginia." The paps surrounded her and she had a panic attack. Dylan thought he'd lost her.

"Or Leia," Fender grumbles.

Leia chased the paps out of town with a shovel. We were away on tour but I wish I had been there. I bet it was glorious.

A reporter points at Jett's forehead. "Can we ask how he got the new scar?"

Jett grins. "You noticed? How sweet."

"What happened?" Another reporter shouts.

"Let me just say this. You can't fight off a shark with a punch to the nose. It's an urban legend."

"You fought with a shark?"

Jett shrugs. "I'm sworn to secrecy."

I chuckle. "Did the shark make you sign an NDA?"

"They're called sharks for a reason."

The DJ from the radio station out of Denver sponsoring today's event stands on a table to gain everyone's attention. "I hope you enjoyed the first portion of today's event. If everyone will proceed to the door, the limos are ready to drive us to lunch."

We retreat to the recording studio while the fans and press leave.

I sigh in relief. "I'm glad we're done."

Jett scowls at me. "You used to enjoy these events. But since you've been dating Mercy, you're boring."

"I'm not boring just because I don't want to sign a woman's pubic."

I shiver. The woman with the boobs was not the last person to disrobe in front of me today. I can't believe I used to enjoy this. There's no challenge when a woman throws herself at you.

But Mercy? Now there's a challenge. And I know the prize is worth the effort since I've had a glimpse of it already.

Chapter 24

Fear — an emotion Mercy didn't realize she'd never felt before today

Mercy

"Uncle Mercury! Your breakfast is ready!" I holler down the hallway.

I frown when he doesn't respond. Usually he's up before me and watching some news program on television. No one needs to watch the news as much as he does.

"Mercury! Come on. No joking around today. I need to get to work."

I check the clock. I really need to get going. A potential client is coming in this morning and I need to prepare. I've never done business with people with enough money to hire someone to restore a car worth more than my annual income before. It's intimidating.

"Mercury," I call again as I walk toward his room. I knock on the door but there's still no answer.

"Are you in the toilet?" If Mercury isn't watching news, he's in the toilet. I spoke to the doctor, but she said it was normal.

"I'm coming in," I warn before opening the door.

Mercury is still in bed. "Time to get up, Uncle Mercury."

He doesn't move. My heart stops at the vision of him lying still in the bed. I rush to him and shake his shoulder.

"Uncle, you okay?"

"Gonna sleep in today, Adhara."

Oh no. He's confused. "It's me, Uncle Mercury."

"Vega, is that you?" His eyes open but they're clouded over. He isn't seeing me. "Vega! It is you. My baby girl has come home."

Who's Vega and what do I do?

"It's not Vega. It's Mercy."

"Stop being silly, Vega. And let me sleep. I'm tired." He rolls over away from me.

I shake his shoulder. "Uncle! Uncle!"

He doesn't respond. I continue to try and wake him but I can't rouse him. Fear latches hold of me. Something's very, very wrong.

I run to the kitchen and snatch my phone from the counter to phone an ambulance. I scream and shout at the emergency services until they assure me an ambulance is on the way.

I rush back to Mercury's room. I clutch his hand. It's warm and his chest moves up and down with his breathing, but he doesn't awaken. Why won't he wake up? What's wrong? Is he dying?

By the time the ambulance arrives, my fear has grown to terror. I can't lose Uncle Mercury. He's my only family.

I refuse to release his hand as the paramedics prepare him for transport. Once he's in the ambulance, I climb in with him. I am not leaving him alone.

I don't know how long the journey to the hospital lasts. I'm too busy staring at the monitors proving Uncle Mercury is alive to pay attention. When the paramedics unload him, I start to follow.

A nurse stops me. "You can't go with them. They need to examine him."

I debate storming past her anyway. She can't stop me. But I don't want to be in the way of the doctors. They need to help Mercury. They need to figure out what's wrong. I can't lose him. I haven't had enough time with him.

I pace the waiting room for what feels like hours before a nurse calls my name. I rush to the desk.

"Yes? Can I see my uncle now? How is he? What happened?"

"They're taking him upstairs. The doctor wants him to stay overnight for observation."

I gulp. Observation isn't bad, is it?

"Can I see him?"

"Third floor. The doctor will meet you in his room to explain once your uncle is settled."

"Thank you," I blurt out before hurrying to the elevators.

Once on the third floor, another nurse directs me to the correct room. I enter to find Mercury sitting up in bed. My knees wobble as relief pours through me. He's okay. Uncle Mercury is not dying today.

"What the hell am I doing here?"

I've never been so happy to hear my grumpy uncle before.

"You wouldn't wake up. You scared the hell out of me."

"Maybe I was tired."

"You thought I was someone named Vega."

He scowls and glances away. I move further into the room until I'm standing next to his bed.

"Who's Vega?"

"My daughter."

Wait. What? He has a daughter? Where is she?

"I can't wait to meet her."

"You can't meet her. She's gone."

Gone as in gone, gone?

I grasp his hand and squeeze. "What happened?"

"She died in the fire with Adhara."

My heart squeezes at the pain in his voice. I didn't know his wife – my great aunt – died in a fire. I want to ask what happened. But I don't dare. The pain in his voice is hard enough to hear.

"I'm sorry, Mercury."

"They were the lights of my life. My stars. Do you know Adhara is a star? Vega, too. The brightest star in the constellation Lyra."

Lyra? My grandmother's name was Lyra. "You named your daughter after my grandmother?"

"Adhara loved her sister something fierce. It didn't matter how Lyra cut us out of her life when we moved to Winter Falls."

"I wish I had known them."

There's a knock on the door and Dr. Vander sashays into the room. "What happened here?"

"I couldn't get him to wake up this morning."

She consults the chart. "It appears Mercury was severely dehydrated."

My brow wrinkles. "But I make sure he has water."

"He's obviously not drinking it."

"Uncle Mercury, you need to drink your fluids," I scold.

"I'll drink when I want to drink," he grumbles.

"You'll drink your fluids or I'll make you wear adult diapers."

He glares at me. "I ain't wearing no diapers."

"Guess you're drinking more water then."

"And you claim I'm crotchety."

"She's right," Dr. Vander says. "If you don't want to end up in the hospital again, you need to drink your fluids."

"I can get you some of those nutritious drinks for the elderly," I tease.

"And I can write you out of my will."

"Go ahead. I don't want your money anyway."

"You're stubborn."

"I thought I was crotchety."

Dr. Vander chuckles. "I'm going to keep you here until tomorrow to make sure your hydration levels are good before sending you home."

"Stupid quack doctors," Mercury mumbles.

"Be nice," I order him.

Dr. Vander shuts the chart and replaces it at the bottom of the bed. "I'll be back for rounds this evening."

As soon as the door shuts behind her, I pick up the remote control and switch on the television.

"I'm not watching news all day," I warn as I click through the channels.

"All day? You're not staying with me all day."

I roll my eyes. "I'm not going home and coming back this evening again. It's a waste of gas."

"Now you understand how to be environmentally conscious?"

I shrug. "When it suits me."

"Don't you have work to do?"

"I cancelled my big meeting. The rest can wait."

"You cancelled your meeting? Why?"

"Maybe because I thought my uncle was on his death bed."

He snorts. "I didn't realize you're such a drama queen."

"When it suits me."

"What about your young man?"

"What about him?"

"Don't you want to spend the day with him?"

I want to spend every second with Gibson. I'm totally becoming obsessed with the man. Becoming? Snort. I am obsessed with the man. I've never felt the way I feel about him before. It's intoxicating. And exciting. And exhilarating.

And scary. What if Gibson doesn't feel the same way about me? What if he's sees me as a challenge? What if he's bored and messing around on me?

"Gibson's busy. He has a meet and greet with fans today."

"Did someone say my name?" Gibson peeks his head in the room. "Can I come in?"

"Yes. And take this one away with you," Mercury says.

Gibson chuckles. "What did she do now?"

I scowl at him. "Hey! No ganging up on the girl!"

Gibson leans over and kisses my cheek. "Hi, sassy girl. You okay?"

"Is she okay?" Mercury asks. "I'm the one laying in the hospital bed."

I sigh. "You're also the one who yelled at me for phoning an ambulance."

"I'm still in the hospital," he grumps.

"How did you know we're here?" I ask as Gibson pulls a chair up next to me.

"I switched on my phone after the meet and greet and it blew up. Everyone in town felt the need to inform me of the situation."

I don't bother asking how everyone knew. The town's gossip network should be used as a model for spy networks. It's beyond good.

"Since you're here you can give this one a ride home." Mercury scowls at me. "She refuses to leave."

"Way to make a girl feel welcome," I mutter.

"I don't need you here insisting I drink water and monopolizing my television."

"What if I need to be here to make sure you don't harass the nurses?"

"I don't harass anyone."

I bark out a laugh. "Liar."

"I'm serious, Mercy. Get out of here. You've been here almost the entire day already."

I glance outside. The sun is waning. It must be late afternoon. I had no idea so much time had passed.

Gibson stands and holds out his hand. "Come on. I'll give you a ride home."

My nose wrinkles. "In an electric car?"

He chuckles as he helps me stand. "I don't have any other choice until my mechanic finishes rebuilding my car."

"Maybe your mechanic is busy."

"Not anymore she isn't," Mercury interrupts. "Get on out of here now."

I kiss his cheek. "I'm glad you're not dead."

"You're still inheriting all my money when I die."

"Not if I drive you crazy first."

Gibson leads me out of the room to the elevator. As soon as the doors close, he pulls me into his arms.

"Are you okay?"

Tears well in my eyes. "No. I thought he was dead."

He rocks me back and forth. "He's not. He's okay. And you're okay, too."

"Thanks for coming for me."

He kisses my hair. "Anything for you, sassy girl. Anything for you."

The line tethering him to me tightens at his words. Gibson is not the man whore I thought he was. He's kind and loving and my heart yearns for him. I hope he doesn't break it.

Chapter 25

Comfort – should be given while not wearing any clothes if Mercy has anything to say about it

GIBSON

I hold Mercy's hand the entire drive from the hospital back to Winter Falls.

"Mercury's tough. He'll be okay," I tell her when I park in front of Mercury's house.

"I know. But he's not getting any younger."

"Neither are we," I joke.

She doesn't laugh. "I just wish I'd known about him years ago. I really hate my mom for keeping my family from me all these years."

I wince. I know how it feels to hate your parents. "Have you spoken to your mom since you arrived in Winter Falls?"

"Nah. She's probably on a bender."

I squeeze her hand. "I'm sorry."

"I guess we both have shitty parents."

Unlike her mom, though, my parents are constantly trying to get in touch with me. I block them, they get another phone number and call me again, and then I block them again. I can't understand what they're thinking.

Why the hell would I want to speak to the people who claimed all the music for *Cash & the Sinners* was written by them and stolen by me? Who claimed they have a right to my money since they paid for my guitar lessons when I was young?

I bought them a house and a car. Made some investments for them. But nothing is good enough. They want it all. Both of them have quit working and live off the investments I made for them but it's not enough. It will never be enough.

"Will you come inside? I don't want to be alone."

The admission costs her. Mercy hates being vulnerable.

"Of course, you don't need to ask."

She nibbles her bottom lip. "What if I'm asking you inside to comfort me?"

I gulp while my cock twitches. It doesn't care how vulnerable Mercy is. It remembers how good it felt to be buried inside her and wants to do it again.

"I don't want to take advantage of you."

"What if I want to take advantage of you?" She winks.

"Don't joke, Mercy."

"Why not? Are you afraid?" She bats her eyelashes.

"I'm afraid you'll regret us having sex in the morning. I don't want to be a regret."

Do I want to be in Mercy's bed? Hell, yeah. But I want to be there because she can't resist me, can't wait for the pleasure I can give her. Not because she's upset about her uncle and needs to forget for a while.

"I won't regret it."

"You said no sex."

"I said no sex *yet*. Yet is over."

"It's only been a few days."

"Okay. I'm just going to say it. This conversation is on the top of the list of conversations I never thought I'd have with Gibson Lewis, guitar player for *Cash & the Sinners*."

She's joking but her words hurt. "I know I haven't always been a gentleman in the past. I've been happy to enjoy the benefits of my fame. But I'm not that man anymore. Not when it comes to you."

Her eyes are full of doubt, so I continue. "I had plenty of opportunity to have sex with fans today. They whipped off their shirts and bras for me." She gasps and I hold up a hand to pre-empt her reply. "I didn't ask them to and I didn't touch any of them. Except to give them autographs. My point is I wasn't the least bit tempted. I am not the same man as I was before we met."

I didn't believe in love before we met. Not since my 'loving' parents sued me when I refused to pay for their membership at the country club.

But now? Mercy's shown me true love does exist. The way she loves her uncle is a good example.

"Now, you're definitely having sex with me."

"What?"

"You can't be all 'I didn't touch the fans because I only want you' and then deny me sex. I'm not allowing it."

I chuckle. "Not allowing it?"

"You heard me." She grabs the door handle. "Get your ass out of this car, march into the house, and have your wicked way with me."

She doesn't wait for my response before jumping out of the car and walking to the door. I chase after her. Of course, I do. There's a limit to how much a sane man can resist this woman and no one's ever accused me of being sane before.

I slam the front door behind me and lock it. Mercy kicks off her cowboy boots before starting to whip off her sweater.

I stop her. "Whoa. Slow down. I'm not fucking you against the wall."

"Why not?" She pouts.

Because I want to show her how much I care for her. I open my mouth to say the words but nothing comes out. The words are stuck in my throat. I can't say them. But I can show her.

I grasp her hand and tug her into my arms. "There's no hurry, sassy girl. We have all night."

"But I want you, guitar man."

I press my hard length against her stomach. "And I want you."

I mold my lips to hers and she immediately opens for me. I groan when her spicy taste hits me. This is what I've been missing. This is what I want. Not some nameless, faceless fan.

I thread my hands through her silky hair and tilt her head so I can dive deeper into her mouth. I want to explore every single inch. Taste every single inch.

She wraps her leg around my waist and rubs her core up and down my length. I slow the kiss before pulling away.

"Bedroom," I growl.

I want to lay her down on a bed where I can touch every inch of her. I want to worship her body with my hands and my tongue. I need to show her how much she means to me. How I'm worth taking a chance on.

She points down the hallway and I throw her over my shoulder.

"Gibson," she shouts as she pounds on my back. "I'm not a damsel in distress."

"Never said you were."

We reach the bedroom. I start to throw her on the bed but stop when I notice the mess of clothes on it.

She groans. "I'm usually not this messy, but I was still in my pajamas when I phoned 911. I had to dress quickly while keeping an eye on Mercury and checking for the arrival of the ambulance."

I set her on her feet. "Stay there."

She frowns. "You're only supposed to order me around when we're naked."

I grin. "I'm glad you agree I'm in charge in the bedroom."

"Damn. I didn't mean—"

I kiss her before she can take back her words.

"I got this," I murmur against her lips before stepping back.

I find the laundry basket and dump her clothes in it. I drop the full basket in the corner of the room before stalking toward Mercy. Her eyes flare as she watches me approach.

"Arms up," I order.

She stares at me for a long moment before slowly lifting her arms. I grasp the hem of her sweater and push it up and off of her leaving her in a simple bra.

I trace the edge of the cup with my finger. Goosebumps explode on her skin and her nipples harden.

"This has to go as well," I growl before reaching behind her and unhooking the bra.

The material falls forward exposing her pretty pink nipples. She shakes her arms and the garment drops to the ground.

"These are mine," I mutter as my hands cover her breasts. I massage and knead them until her head falls back and she rubs her legs together.

I draw my hands down her sides to the waistband of her jeans.

"Why did you stop?" she whines.

"I need these off."

She reaches for the button but I slap her hands away. "My job."

"Get to it, guitar man."

I nip her shoulder. "Are you impatient?"

"Maybe I'm not impatient. Maybe you're slow."

"I'm slow?"

"As molasses."

I rip her jeans open and I wedge my hand under her panties until I find her pussy and spear her with two fingers. Her inner muscles ripple around my fingers.

"Is this slow?" I ask as I pump my fingers in and out of her.

She groans.

I freeze. "You didn't answer me."

She lifts her chin and glares at me. "You stopped again."

"I'll stop as many times as I want if you can't learn to listen to me."

Her eyes narrow. "If you want a woman who listens to you, you're in the wrong bedroom."

I smirk. "You love it when I order you around in the bedroom and you know it."

"I know no such thing."

"Remove your panties and jeans but keep me inside you the entire time," I order.

Her eyes flare. Yep. She loves it when I order her around in the bedroom. But I'm not going to argue with her about it. My patience is up. My cock is hard and leaking. I'm ready to lay her down on the bed and show her how good we are together. Show her what she means to me.

She pushes her jeans and panties down her hips. When the material is at her knees, she stops. She glances around the room as if searching for a solution.

She shackles my wrist and squeezes tight as she shifts backward until she hits the bed. She sits while keeping a tight grip on my wrist. She pushes her jeans to her ankles and kicks them off.

"I'm completely naked. There's no one home. What are you going to do to me?" She flutters her eyelashes at me.

"Whatever I want," I growl before I resume pumping my fingers in and out of her.

She widens her legs and begins to ride my fingers.

"There you go, sassy girl. Take what you need."

I press my heel against her clit as I continue to work her. She moans and her hands lift to play with her breasts.

"You are the sexiest thing I've ever seen." My eyes are glued to the way she plays with herself.

It's not long before her walls tighten on my fingers.

"Come for me, sassy girl. Come all over my fingers."

"Yes," she breathes.

"Say my name when you come."

She lifts her head and her eyes meet mine. "Gibson," she groans as her climax hits.

I continue to pump in and out of her until she collapses on the bed. I remove my fingers before licking them clean. Spicy. She tastes spicy everywhere. I debate getting to my knees and tasting her pussy but my cock's patience is gone.

I lift Mercy up and place her in the middle of the bed before quickly stripping. I dig a condom out of my wallet and don it before joining her on the bed.

"Think you can handle another round?"

Her eyes light with challenge. "Think you can?"

I lay next to her. "Get on me."

She straddles me but I twirl my finger. "Other way around. I want to watch your ass while you take me."

Her eyes flare and her breath hitches. I twirl my finger again and she nods before whirling around until I have the perfect view of her lean back, wide hips, and luscious ass.

"Lift yourself up and put my cock inside you."

"Bossy," she mutters but does as I say.

Once I'm notched at her entrance, she slowly lowers herself down. I dig my fingers into her hips and grit my teeth to stop myself from coming.

Mercy is some kind of witch. Or maybe a magician. No other woman has made me want to come at the first stroke. But being inside her isn't the same as being inside any other woman. This is heaven. Pure and simple.

"Ride me," I growl.

She braces her hands on my thighs before lifting and lowering herself on me. I was wrong. *This* is heaven. Watching her take me.

I use my hold on her hips to increase her pace until our skins slap together. My balls draw up but I grit my teeth and hold on. I'm not coming before my sassy girl.

I wind one hand around her hip to find her clit. I press against it and rub circles the way I know she prefers. Her pace increases in response.

"Play with those pretty titties, sassy girl. Make yourself come all over my cock."

"I'm… I'm…"

"Come, Mercy," I order.

Her head falls back and she shouts, "Gibson."

Her climax triggers mine. "Mercy," I grind out as she continues to bounce up and down on my cock.

When her orgasm wanes, she collapses forward on my legs. I sit up and pull her into my arms. My chest to her back. I kiss her neck.

"I…"

I pause. I was about to say I love you. What the hell? I don't love Mercy. I admit I'm falling for her. But I'm not there yet. Or am I?

She giggles. "I made you speechless."

Yeah, she did.

Chapter 26

Bossy – a personality trait Mercy claims to hate. She's lying.

MERCY

I snuggle into the warmth behind me, and Gibson's arms tighten around me.

"You're still here," I murmur.

He kisses my neck. "I'm still here."

I glance over my shoulder at him. "What happened? Did you pass out?"

"I didn't pass out. But you did." He wiggles his eyebrows.

I kick his shin. "I did not pass out."

"Sure, you didn't."

"And you can't distract me. Why are you still here?"

"Why wouldn't I be?"

I roll my eyes. "Because you don't enjoy sleeping with women."

He presses his hard length against my ass. "I think I proved to you how much I enjoy sleeping with women."

"I don't mean sex. I mean sleeping, sleeping." I feign snoring.

"Are you saying I snore?"

He totally snores but I'm done with him distracting me. I roll over to face him.

"Why are you here, Gibson? Here in this bed with me. The morning after."

He pushes the hair off of my face. "Because this is real, sassy girl. We're the real deal. This isn't fake anymore, remember?"

"Good answer. I give it an eight out of ten," I sass because I can't handle him being sweet. I'm afraid if he's any sweeter to me I won't be falling in love anymore. I will have fallen. And I'm not ready. The risk is too great.

"What do I have to do to get a ten?"

I bite my bottom lip and pretend to contemplate his question.

"Come on, Mercy. Give me a ten."

He tickles my ribs and I bat him away but he's determined. He rolls on top of me and I feel his hard length press against my core. I moan. I don't care how many times he woke me up last night, my body is a slut for this man.

He thrusts against me and since there's hardly any barrier between us I can feel how hard and hot he is. I wrap my legs around his waist and rub myself against him.

My phone rings and I jolt.

"Saved by the bell," Gibson mutters before rolling off of me. "Answer your phone. It could be the hospital."

The hospital? Shit. I forgot about my uncle.

"I can go pick Uncle Mercury up," I say after I hang up the phone.

"Let me get dressed and I'll drive you."

"You don't need to drive me."

"Mercy." He palms my neck to draw me near and kisses my forehead. "I'm driving you. End of story."

"Bossy."

He growls. "You enjoy it when I'm bossy."

"Whatever," I grumble since he's right. Gibson bossy in the bedroom is the hottest thing I've ever experienced in my life.

"Get dressed. I'll make coffee."

He jumps out of bed. Stark naked. I watch as he roams around the bedroom. His body is a thing of beauty – all those lean muscles covered in ink.

"What do your tattoos mean?"

I've licked those tattoos, followed the outlines with my fingers, but I want to know what they mean. Gibson was too busy moaning to answer my questions about his ink last night.

He puts on his jeans before answering. "I'm not Dylan. There's no deep meaning to my tattoos. Most of them I got after a night out with Jett."

He slaps my ass. "Now, get moving. We need to pick up your uncle before he pisses off the entire hospital and gets banned."

I snort. "You're delirious if you think he hasn't already pissed off the entire staff of the hospital."

Fifteen minutes later we're driving away from the house.

"I still don't understand why we're driving this thing instead of the Charger," I complain as Gibson drives.

"This is roomier. And easier for Mercury to climb into."

This being the Hummer Gibson borrowed from Fender. On top of an electric engine, it's a big block I worry will tip over if we take a corner too fast.

But Gibson's right. My uncle will have more room in here than the backseat of the Charger. Still. Being responsible is boring.

"I'll park and meet you in his room," Gibson says as he pulls up to the entrance of the hospital.

I lean over the console and kiss him. "Thanks."

I jump out of the car and am nearly at Uncle Mercury's room when I realize I kissed him in thanks without a second thought. I'm not usually a woman who gives out affection without thinking. What is Gibson doing to me?

"Finally!" Uncle Mercury shouts when I arrive at his room and my worries about Gibson and the possibility he's a wizard fly out of my mind. "It's about time you came back to spring me from jail."

"Did you forget you kicked me out of your room yesterday?"

"I don't need no one hovering over me."

"I think you meant to say: *Thank you, Mercy, for bringing me to the hospital and waiting while the doctors examined you.*"

"Here we are," a nurse says as she enters the room with a wheelchair.

Mercury scowls at the wheelchair. "I don't need a wheelchair."

"You can't leave the hospital without one."

"This is some bullshit."

"Uncle Mercury!" I warn. "Be nice to her. She's only following the rules."

"Rules are made to be broken."

"Right on," Gibson says as he enters the room.

I scowl at him. "Not helping."

He shrugs. "Don't act as if you're suddenly a rule follower now. I thought you were going to break a tooth with how hard you were grinding your teeth when I slowed down to the speed limit in town."

The nurse giggles. "I love families."

I open my mouth to contradict her. To tell her we're not a family. Gibson isn't part of our family. But I shut my mouth when I realize I want him to be. I want him to support me and stand behind me when Uncle Mercury is being grumpy.

I want him in my life period. I want to spend my days with him. Grow old with him. Argue with him when we're old and gray and can barely remember our names.

Welp. I've gone and done it. I've fallen in love with my guitar man. My heart pounds, sweat beads on my forehead, and my hands shake. This is either the first mile on Heartbreak Highway or the start of something amazing.

I glance over at Gibson who's laughing with Uncle Mercury. I blow out a breath and let the tension roll off of me. I am not going to start this relationship with worries about what if. I'm in love with Gibson, and I'm giving our relationship my all. No overthinking allowed.

Gibson pushes the wheelchair in front of my uncle. "Your chariot awaits, sir."

"Don't need no chariot."

"Maybe not but you've also never been given a ride by a rockstar before."

I gasp. He's not supposed to tell the world he's a rockstar. The hospital will be inundated with press.

The nurse pats my shoulder. "Don't worry. The entire hospital realized he was the guitarist for *Cash & the Sinners* yesterday."

My brow furrows. "Does everyone know who *Cash & the Sinners* is?"

Gibson chuckles. "Everyone except you because you have no taste in music."

I plant my hands on my hips. "There is nothing wrong with country music. You hummed to my music in the car the other day."

"Because the song reminded me of one of ours."

"You're impossible."

He waggles his eyebrows. "And you love it."

I do. I also love him. But I bite my tongue and keep the words to myself.

"Whatever," I mumble. "Are we blowing this popsicle stand or what?"

Everyone's attention focuses on Uncle Mercury who's scowling at the wheelchair as if it personally did him wrong.

I sigh and pull my phone out of my pocket. "I guess I'll contact Basil and let him know I won't be in today."

Mercury wags a finger at me. "You are going to work today, young lady."

I motion to the wheelchair. "I can't go to work if I'm stuck in the hospital all day because someone is being stubborn."

"I'm not stubborn."

"And I'm not planning to steal your Dodge Charger."

Mercury huffs as he lowers himself in the wheelchair. "You don't have to steal it. It's yours when I die."

"I told you. I am not accepting your money."

"You can't give it back. I'll be dead."

I frown. I don't want Uncle Mercury to die. I need more time with him. But yesterday showed me how fragile he is. I need to cherish every moment I have with him and stop being angry at Mom for keeping his existence a secret. Easier said than done.

"What the hell's this thing?" Mercury asks when we reach the Hummer.

I high-five him. "Exactly what I thought."

Gibson chuckles. "You two are like peas in a pod."

"I don't eat peas," Mercury says.

"And we all know what happens when I eat peas." Gibson winks at me. I don't think he's referring to the green vegetables I added to the pasta.

Mercury tries to stand but he's still weak from being dehydrated. Gibson frowns before scooping him up and placing him in the backseat.

"I don't need your help," Mercury shouts after Gibson as he returns the wheelchair to the hospital.

"Sure, you didn't!" Gibson shouts back.

"I don't know if I like your young man," Mercury grumbles.

I know I don't like him. I love him. The words still scare the hell out of me but I've never let fear stop me before. Why start now?

Gibson climbs into the car and smiles over at me. "Ready?"

Yep. I'm ready for whatever happens next. Fingers crossed it's not a stop at the Heartbreak Hotel. That place has fleas and the sheets are threadbare.

Chapter 27

Phone call – a trigger for the downfall

GIBSON

"What are you doing here?" Jett asks when I enter the house we're renting together.

"I live here or have you forgotten since you hit your head?"

He scowls. "Being injured is boring. I'm supposed to 'rest'. No parachuting. No rock climbing. No parkouring. No bungee jumping. What am I supposed to do? I'm bored."

Uh oh. A bored Jett is not good. The last time he was bored he decided to enter a Via Ferrata competition. You'd think traversing a mountain via ladders, cables, and bridges would be right up his alley. It was. As was drinking beer while doing the competition. Ladders and a drunk Jett are not a good combo.

"Why don't we play Grand Theft Auto?" I suggest.

I don't have anything better to do than play games with Jett today either. Not when Mercy is working and we have no band obligations.

Jett rubs his hands together. "I'm going to kick your ass."

"You can try."

My stomach growls a few hours later and I check the clock. "I need a break."

"Pussy," Jett mutters but he pauses the game. "What are we going to eat? Fender hasn't filled our fridge for days."

"Let's eat at the brewery."

"The diner's open."

I scowl at him. "I'm not going to fall off the wagon and drink just because we have lunch at the brewery."

He studies me for a moment before sighing. "Fine. But I'm not accepting any responsibility for what happens."

I grab a jacket and we head out.

"Should we ask Fender to join us?" I ask as we pass the house he shares with Leia.

Jett snorts. "I walked in on him and Leia once. I don't need a repeat."

I shove his shoulder. "Liar. You stood there and watched."

He shrugs. "It was hot as hell. Always handy to have some material for my spank bank."

"Women still rejecting your advances?" I tease as we continue walking to the brewery.

He glares at me. "I can have any woman I want."

Except there's only one woman he wants but he refuses to give in to her. Poor Aurora is in for a long wait while Jett grows up and realizes love is worth taking a chance on.

I nearly stumble at my thoughts. A mere two months ago Jett and I thought the same. We even agreed to a pact – neither one of us would fall in love. But now here I am thinking he's an idiot.

It's confirmed. Mercy can wield magic.

Cayenne waves as she approaches. "How are you boys doing?"

Jett hitches up his pants. "We're not boys."

She giggles. "No, you are not." She winks at him before addressing me, "How is Mercy holding up?"

"She's okay. A bit shaken but you know Mercy. Strong as the cars she repairs."

She pats my shoulder. "We'll keep a better eye on Mercury from now on. The little sneak must have been pouring his drinks into a plant."

"Much appreciated," I say and she continues on her way.

"What happened to Old Man Mercury?" Jett asks.

I fill him in as we reach Main Street and turn toward *Naked Falls Brewing.* Clove rushes out of her coffee shop, *Clove's Coffee Corner,* and waves us down.

"How is Mercury?" she asks when we reach her.

I chuckle. "Like you haven't heard from Cayenne already."

"You're starting to get the hang of small town living."

I am. Winter Falls is the shit. I never thought I'd want to live somewhere where everyone knows my name but the town residents are quirky and fun.

Several tourists walk into her café. "Give Mercy our love," she says as she hurries off to help them.

"You're fitting into town," Jett says.

It's not a compliment. It's an accusation. There's not enough adventure to be found in Winter Falls for him. If he'd stop running away from his past, he'd realize he doesn't need to chase adventure.

"It's a cool town." I point to Forest who's walking his chipmunks without any pants on.

Jett chuckles. "You may have a point."

We reach the brewery and are immediately shown to a table in the corner.

"There are some tourists in here," the waitress says. "Better to stay a bit hidden." She narrows her eyes on me. "Unless you're going to hit on them."

I raise my hands. "Not me. I'm taken." I motion to Jett. "He might be interested, though."

Jett frowns. "I'm supposed to be taking it easy."

Taking it easy has never stopped him from charming a fan into his bed before. He uses sex like a drug. When he isn't consuming actual drugs. Although, he doesn't do drugs around us anymore. Not after the great mushroom debacle.

"You doing okay?" I ask once we've ordered and the waitress has left us alone.

He taps his forehead. "Do you need to ask?"

"I meant mentally. You're not interested in chasing after female fans and you were moping around this morning."

He drums his fingers on the table. "Just bored. Ready to get on tour again."

Before Mercy, I felt the same way. Anxious to hit the road, to play big venues, have the fans scream at me. But not anymore.

I miss the music. But the rest? Being exhausted all the time? Unable to sleep on a moving bus? Waking up not knowing what city I'm in? Nah.

My phone buzzes in my pocket. Usually, I ignore it. But maybe it's Mercy. Maybe she's done with work early. Excitement fizzles in my blood.

I don't glance at the caller before answering. "Hey! Missing me?"

"Son," my dad begins and my blood boils. How did he get this number? Why won't he leave me alone?

"No. I don't want to hear it."

"Don't make me sue you again."

I growl. "Sue me all you want. You'll never win."

"Son," he begins again.

"I am not your son."

"I saw you born in the hospital, I raised you until you left for college, I paid for your guitar lessons for years."

Here we go again. He paid for the guitar lessons and thus he has a right to all of my earnings. Never mind I'm the one who played those strings until my fingers bled. Never mind I'm the one who shared a studio apartment with four other men to save money. Never mind how I survived on noodles and day old pizza for years until we got our first record deal.

My dad and mom are the ones who suffered. Not me and my bandmates.

"You haven't been answering my calls."

"Probably because I don't want to speak to you."

"You are my son. You will answer me when I call," he demands.

We could go around in circles for days. I'm not interested. I haven't been interested in years. Not since the first time a process server announced *You've been served.*

"What do you want?"

"We need help getting the car fixed."

I massage my temple where I feel a headache coming on. "What's wrong with the Mercedes?"

"It's old."

"Old? I bought you the Mercedes less than five years ago."

"Exactly. It's old."

"I'm not buying you a new car because you think a five-year-old Mercedes is beneath you."

What happened to my parents? We grew up in a middle-class neighborhood. My dad was an electrician with his own business and my mom an office manager. I never wanted for anything growing up. We had enough.

So when *Cash & the Sinners* hit the top of the charts for the first time, I bought them a bigger house in a fancy neighborhood as a token of my appreciation for giving me everything I needed as a child. But since then, they've never had enough. How did I miss their greed? Their desire to have it all but not work for it?

"You will buy us a new car or we'll sue."

"Yeah? How did that work out for you last time?"

"Pretty well."

Damn it. I should have never settled the case. I shouldn't have listened to our manager who was worried about the band's reputation. I should have fought them. Because now they think I'm a cash machine. They ring, and I dispense money.

I am done giving them money. I've been done giving them money for a while.

"Fine. Sue me. While the case is in court, I'll stop your allowance." And then I'll make sure my lawyers delay and delay until my parents have to sell their 'old' Mercedes for money.

"This isn't how a son should treat his parents."

"Because suing a son for more money when you're already living off him is how parents are supposed to treat their son?" I fire back.

"You don't understand."

"I understand perfectly. You and mom are greedy and lazy. I can't believe you're the same parents who raised me."

I hang up the phone and block the number before slamming it on the table.

"I can't believe those assholes."

Jett shrugs. "They're your parents."

My nostrils flare and I fist my hands before I reach across the table and strangle him. His outlook on the situation is completely different than mine. Considering his background, it's understandable. But he could support me for a change.

"Everything okay?" The waitress asks when she arrives and places our meals in front of us.

"Can I get a beer?" I ask.

She smiles. "Coming right up. Enjoy your meals."

"Gibson," Jett growls.

I throw up a hand. "No. I won't have you dictating my life. Besides, it's only one beer."

Chapter 28

Bitch – a name you should never call Mercy

MERCY

I hesitate at the door to Gibson's house. We agreed we'd meet up tonight but I haven't heard from him since before lunch. Am I being a stage five clinger by coming to his house this way?

Whenever I'd question Zeke where he was when we were dating and he wouldn't answer his phone for hours, he'd claim I was clinging. He couldn't breathe because I was suffocating him.

I scowl. I'm not a clinger. Zeke was an asshole. He said I was a clinger to avoid telling me where he was because he was a big fat cheater.

Gibson isn't Zeke. He's kind and considerate.

I raise my hand to knock, but the door flies open before I can.

"I was wondering how long you were going to stand there," Jett says.

I narrow my eyes at him. "I was thinking."

He steps out onto the porch and shuts the door behind him. Alarm bells go off in my head. Why is he stopping me from entering the house he shares with Gibson?

"I need to prepare you."

Those alarm bells are blaring now. My heart pounds as fear races through me. Is Gibson with another woman? Is he cheating on me? I clutch my chest. "What's going on?"

Jett scratches his chin. "Um…"

"Tell me already." The suspense is killing me.

"We went to the brewery for lunch."

"And?" I push.

"And um…"

"This is not you preparing me. This is you freaking me out."

"Mercy!" Gibson shouts from within the house.

"Damn," Jett mutters before he opens the door and motions for me to enter. "I'll be somewhere else. Fender is next door if you need him."

"Why would I need Fender?"

He shrugs as he retreats to the porch steps.

"And where are you going?"

He waves. What he doesn't do is answer.

"Mercy!"

I inhale a deep breath and march into the house. Whatever the problem is I can handle it.

I find Gibson laying on the sofa in the living room.

"You're here!" He attempts to stand but stumbles and ends up rolling off the sofa onto the floor. He laughs. "Oops!"

"Are you drunk?" I ask.

Here I thought he was hollering for me because something was wrong and he needed me. Not hardly.

"Drunk? Nah. I just had a few beers."

I wait until he manages to sit up and lean against the sofa before speaking. "A few beers?"

"At the brewery."

I contemplate how to respond. I know accusing him isn't the way to go. "You promised not to drink while we're dating."

"It was only a few beers."

I'm not an idiot. I know the difference between someone who's had a few beers and someone who's drunk off his ass. With my experience I could write a dissertation paper on the difference.

"If it was only a few beers, why are you lying on the floor?"

He staggers to his feet and stumbles toward me. He attempts to throw his arms around me but I step out of his reach. He sways to the side and I catch him before he falls.

"Come on. Let's sit on the sofa." I wrap an arm around his waist and help him to the sofa. Good thing I have lots of experience moving drunk people because he does not make it easy for me. Coordination is not his friend right now.

"You had more than a few beers," I accuse as I stand above him.

"What's the big deal? It was only a bit of comfort."

I know better than to ask but I do anyway. "Why did you need comfort?"

He scowls and reaches for the beer on the coffee table. I swipe it before he can grab it.

"Dad called. He wants more money."

"And you decided to have a drink to make you feel better after you talked to him."

"I knew you'd understand."

I understand all too well.

"And how many beers did you have?"

He shrugs. The movement causes him to pitch to his side. He might not be slurring his words but he's clearly drunk.

I eye the door. I can go home and come back tomorrow when he's sober. But I'm not a chicken. And tomorrow the situation will be the same.

I sit on the coffee table and place a hand on his thigh.

"You have a problem, guitar man."

"Yeah, my dad's an asshole."

He's not wrong but I'm not discussing his dad now. "I meant your unhealthy attitude with alcohol."

"I'm not an alcoholic. I'm not your mom. I had a few beers. What's the big deal?"

I inhale a deep breath and try again. "You had more than a few beers and you promised me you wouldn't drink."

"I didn't promise to never drink again."

"You promised not to drink while we're dating."

His nose wrinkles. "The whole time we're dating?"

This is a waste of time. I know better than to try and reason with a drunk. Reasoning with a drunk person is more difficult than convincing a kid chocolate's bad for them. Either way. It's a complete and utter waste of time.

"Yes, the whole time."

I stand. I'm wasting my time here. Gibson isn't going to listen to me now. I gather the beers on the table and march to the kitchen.

"What are you doing?"

I don't answer as I open each can one by one and pour the contents down the drain.

"You can't throw away my beer."

I don't answer him. I place the cans in the recycling bin before turning around. It's time for me to go home.

"Where do you think you're going?" He asks when I reach the door.

"Home. I'll see you tomorrow."

"Are you fucking kidding me? You throw away my beer and then walk away? What the hell, Mercy?"

"Fender is next door. I'll ask him to keep an eye on you."

"I'm not a child. I don't need anyone to keep an eye on me."

"Okay." It might sound as if I'm agreeing, but I'm not. I'm still warning Fender Gibson's drunk and alone.

"Will you stop being a bitch?"

I cringe at the word bitch. I freaking hate the word. It's a trigger for me since my mom loved to scream at me for being a bitch whenever I tried to help her get sober.

"What did you call me?"

He doesn't hesitate. "Bitch."

Oh goodie. We've reached the nasty drunk portion of the evening.

"Please don't call me the b-word."

"Bitch."

I was wrong. I can't do this. I can't handle this problem.

"I love you, but I can't do this."

"If you loved me, you wouldn't be a bitch to me."

Tears well in my eyes but I sniff and hold them back. I will not cry in front of Gibson. I will not let him see how his words are killing me.

I open the door. "Goodbye, Gibson."

"Where are you going? You need to buy me more beer since you threw away the ones I bought. Don't you dare leave me here!"

I slam the door. I can't listen to this.

"Mercy!" Leia hollers from the house next door.

I wave at her and turn in the opposite direction. I can't talk to her now. Not when my heart is breaking.

"Mercy!" She hollers again. "Don't make me chase you."

I increase my pace as the first tears fall down my face. I don't want anyone to see me this way. Especially not my new friend who has a perfect life with her perfect rockstar.

My perfect rockstar was an illusion. I knew better than to fall for him. I knew I should have kept my heart encased behind a brick wall.

But what did I do? I fell for his charm. I believed I could be a rockstar's girlfriend.

When will I learn my lesson? I need to start making better decisions about men.

Forget that. I need to stay away from men period. End of sentence.

I don't need a man. I have my business, my uncle, and my friends. I don't need anything more.

Chapter 29

Wake up call – something Gibson is in dire need of

GIBSON

"Wake up, asshole!" Jett shouts before kicking my feet.

"Fuck off," I say as I roll over.

The mattress tilts to the side and I find myself crashing to the floor. I open my eyes to glare at Jett but he's not alone. Fender is holding the mattress while Cash, Dylan, and Jett glare at me.

"What the hell is your problem?"

"Get dressed. We need to talk," Cash orders before marching out of the room.

Fender grunts and drops the mattress back in place on the bed before following him out.

Dylan glowers at me. "You brought this on yourself."

I wait until Jett and I are alone before speaking again. "Did you tattletale on me?"

He crosses his arms over his chest. "You have a problem. You need to deal with it."

I get to my feet. "My only problem is my bandmates are a bunch of meddling bastards who keep poking their noses in my business."

He sighs. "We care about you. We're your family."

"You have a funny way of showing it."

"Whatever. Get dressed. We'll be downstairs."

I wait until he closes the door behind him before sinking onto the bed. Damn. My head hurts. My stomach gurgles. How much did I drink yesterday? I remember speaking to my dad and ordering a beer at the brewery. And then I bought a case of twenty-four beers before coming home and drinking the rest of it.

Except for the beers Mercy emptied down the kitchen drain. I frown. Mercy. I remember her stopping by but it's all kind of fuzzy. She's probably pissed I broke my promise not to drink.

I better apologize to her. I snatch my phone from the night stand and send her a message.

> *Sorry about yesterday.*

I tap my foot as I wait for her to answer. I check the time. She's probably at work and can't answer.

I throw on a pair of jeans and sweatshirt before making my way downstairs. I might as well get this bullshit with the band over in the meantime.

My bandmates are waiting for me in the living room. Fender is standing guard in front of the door with his arms crossed over his chest. Jett is pacing the floor. And Cash and Dylan are sitting on the couch whispering. They immediately stop when I walk in.

I ignore them and continue to the kitchen. I rummage in the drawers for some painkillers. I pop two in my mouth and swallow them with a glass of water. I hope these work quickly because I don't want to deal with my band with this headache.

I take my time finding a mug and pouring a coffee. I debate making myself breakfast but my stomach rebels at the idea.

"Are you done delaying?" Cash asks when I enter the living room.

I shrug as I plop down on a chair.

"The band is officially on break," Dylan declares.

I rub a hand through my hair. What is going on here?

"What the hell do you mean? We have a new record out. Our next single is dropping soon. We need to promote it. And we have a tour planned."

"Dylan is being nice," Cash says.

"What he means," Jett continues before Cash can. "Is you're out of the band until you get clean."

I rear back. "Get clean? I'm not an addict. I'm not the one who tried mushrooms and nearly caused our bus to crash."

Jett grits his teeth. "And what happened when I came down? I agreed to never ingest mushrooms again."

"I never agreed to not drink again."

Jett raises his eyebrow. "But you did promise Mercy you wouldn't drink."

I snort. "Are you serious? You're bringing up my agreement with Mercy when you don't even like her?"

"I like her well enough."

"Which is why you bring up our pact not to fall in love every time she's around."

"I can like Mercy but be mad at you for breaking our pact at the same time."

"Since when can you multi-task?"

"Guys," Cash interrupts. "We're getting off topic here."

"What is the topic? Oh right. The topic is how you're a bunch of assholes who want to kick me out of the band because I had a few beers yesterday after my dad called."

"Fuck," Dylan mutters. "You didn't tell us his dad called."

Jett glances away, but not before there's a flash of guilt in his eyes. He deliberately kept the information about my dad to himself. "Does it matter?"

Dylan frowns. "Of course it matters. We could have been more gentle with him."

"Being gentle isn't going to work. He needs his ass kicked," Jett says.

"And you're the one who's going to do it?" I chuckle.

Jett points to Fender. "No, he will."

I glance over my shoulder at Fender. "You would really hit me?"

"I tried to help you," he grumbles. "I'm out of options."

"Help me? Hiding my beer wasn't helping me."

Cash clears his throat. "Can we stop going around in circles? This isn't getting us anywhere."

I jump to my feet. My temples throb and my stomach revolts but I ignore the pain. It's nothing compared to the pain of the only family I have left abandoning me.

"I can't believe all of you. You're supposed to be my family. And this is how you treat me? Kick me out because I'm not behaving in the manner you want me to?"

Dylan sighs and stands before approaching me. "You have a problem, Gibson. We're out of options here. Go into rehab and get sober or you're out."

"Why the hell would I go into rehab? I'm not an alcoholic."

"You ruined your relationship with the woman you love for a few beers," Dylan claims.

I frown. "I didn't ruin my relationship with Mercy."

He cocks an eyebrow. "The girls are with Mercy now while she cries her eyes out because you broke her heart."

"I didn't break her heart. We argued about my drinking and she left."

His face softens. "Gibson, you called her a bitch."

"I wouldn't call Mercy a bitch."

"She asked you to not use the word and you called her a bitch again. She said she loves you and you called her a bitch."

I shake my head. "No, this isn't right."

Mercy never said she loves me. I would remember her saying those words. I would remember the woman I'm falling for declaring her love for me. And there's no way I would call her a bitch. No way.

"I don't believe you."

I walk away while digging my phone out of my pocket. Fender blocks my path to the front porch so I make my way to the back patio instead. I dial Mercy's number. When she answers on the first ring, relief fills me. I knew it wasn't as bad as Dylan made out.

"This is Mercy's phone."

"Virginia? Why are you answering Mercy's phone?"

"Because she doesn't want to speak to you."

My stomach falls. Is Dylan right? Did I say those horrible things to Mercy? I need to make this right. I can't lose her. I love her.

I wait for the freak out those three words should cause but it doesn't come. Instead, peace settles over me. I love Mercy. She's the woman I've been waiting for. And apparently I treated her worse than crap yesterday. Shit.

"I need to apologize," I tell Virginia. I'll beg if I have to. I'll do whatever's necessary.

"Hold on."

I pace the porch as I wait for Mercy to come to the phone.

"Gibson?"

I frown. "Indigo, where's Mercy? I want to speak to her. I don't want to play phone tag."

"You're stuck with me. Virginia is trying to calm Mercy down."

"Calm her down? Why does she need to be calmed down? Is Uncle Mercury okay?"

"Old Man Mercury is fine. He's going to outlive us all. You, on the other hand, are going to be dead if Mercy gets her hands on you."

I can't blame her. I know she hates the word bitch. It's what her mother calls her whenever Mercy tries to help get her sober.

My stomach flips. I didn't mess up yesterday. I completely and totally fucked up.

"Let me apologize to her."

"What do you want to apologize for?"

I blow out a breath. "For how I treated her yesterday."

"And how did you treat her yesterday?"

"Not very well."

She sighs. "You don't remember, do you?"

Shit. This is bad. I open my mouth to lie but stop. Lying is not the way to make this right. "Dylan told me."

"I'm sorry, Gibson, but it's not a good idea for you to speak with her now." Indigo hangs up before I have a chance to argue with her.

I scream and launch the phone across the yard before falling to my knees. What am I going to do? Mercy is never going to forgive me for a drunken rant. Not with her history. She hates drunks and for good reason.

I've lost her. I've lost the best thing to ever happen to me in my life. Better than meeting my bandmates. Better than getting our first number one hit. Better than female fans throwing themselves at me.

None of *that* matters. Mercy does.

I need to win her back. I can't live without her. But how?

There's only one way I can think of to even have a remote chance of getting her back. I stand and march back into the house.

"What's the plan?" I ask.

Jett grins. "I told you threatening to kick him out of the band would work."

"Asshole, I don't give a shit about the band. I need to win Mercy back."

"There's a private clinic about two hours away. They're expecting you today. Fender will drive you," Cash says.

"What about the band? And the publicity?"

Dylan snorts. "Mike is eating this shit up."

Figures our manager would find a way to turn my visit to rehab into a marketing opportunity.

"You ready?" I ask Fender.

"Whenever you are."

I motion to the door he's still guarding. "Let's go."

"You don't want to pack a bag?" Cash asks.

"I'm good." I point to Jett. "Try not to get into too much trouble while I'm gone."

He grins. "Who me?"

I say goodbye to Cash and Dylan and then it's time to go.

Chapter 30

Unicorn's tears – don't exist since unicorns never cry unlike Mercy after getting her heart broken

Mercy

"Ouch!" I drop the wrench on the floor and lift my finger to my mouth to suck the blood before using my feet to roll myself out from under the engine.

This is not me. I don't make stupid mistakes and cut myself while working on an engine. But my mind isn't on rebuilding this classic V8 engine. I keep hearing Gibson calling me a bitch over and over again in my mind. I told him I loved him and he didn't respond.

I hang my head. What was I thinking? Thinking I could be a rockstar's girlfriend and not end up with my heart shattered. My relationship losing streak continues. Too bad there isn't a prize for this streak.

My phone rings and I glance at the display. *Gibson.*

He's lost his damn mind if he thinks I'm talking to him today. I already know everything he has to say. *I didn't mean it. I won't drink again. It was a bad day.* Yada yada yada. I've heard all of the excuses he can come up with. I'm not interested.

Virginia rushes in the garage with Indigo and Leia hot on her heels.

"I got it." Virginia picks up my phone and answers, "This is Mercy's phone."

"What are you doing here?" I ask Indigo and Leia.

Indigo rolls her eyes. "She doesn't get small town living."

"Or maybe she doesn't get having the nosiest woman in town think she's her bestie," Leia says.

Indigo holds up a finger. "One, I am her bestie." She holds up another finger. "And, two, I can't possibly be the nosiest woman in town when the gossip gals live here."

"Mercy?" Virginia waves my phone at me. "It's he whose name shall not be spoken. Do you want to listen to him grovel?"

I growl. Does Gibson actually think I'm going to listen to him? What a tool. "No. I already know every word he's going to say. I'm not interested."

"Don't you want to give him a piece of your mind?" Leia asks.

Huh. Not a bad idea. There's no reason for me to slink away all heartbroken. I'm not some forlorn heroine in a romance novel.

I hold out my hand. "Give me the phone."

Indigo snatches it from Virginia before I can. "Gibson?"

I wave my hand at her and mouth *give me the phone.*

Indigo grins and shakes her head. "You're stuck with me. Virginia is trying to calm Mercy down."

"Whatever," I mutter and stomp off to the bathroom where I wash my cut with some water and put a bandage on it.

"Let's go." Indigo motions to the door when I return to the garage.

"I have work to do."

Basil steps out of his office. "Get out of here before you burn the place down."

I scowl. "I wouldn't burn this place down." I just bought it. I haven't even had a chance to get insurance yet.

He nods to my bandage. "I wouldn't expect you to cut yourself either."

I'm allowed to be a bit distracted the day after the man I love – the man I thought I'd spend my life with – breaks my heart. But I'm not going to tell him my sad story. I've spent my life working in garages with men. They don't care about my 'women' troubles. I stick my tongue out at him instead.

"Seriously. Get out of here. This rebuild isn't going to be finished today anyway."

"Isn't this your garage?" Leia asks. "Aren't you the boss now?"

"My garage. Basil's client."

"Enough chitter chatter." Indigo laces her arm through mine. "Let's go."

"Where are we going?" I ask.

"My house. And don't worry. Cash won't be there."

"Where is he?" I ask because wherever Cash is, Gibson is, and I can't help but wonder what he's doing. Does he have the hangover of the century or is he already drinking again?

No, Mercy. Stop it. No thinking about rockstars and wondering how they're doing. It's no longer any of your business.

Indigo pats my arm. "I'll explain later."

Explain what? Now, I'm even more curious. Nope. I don't care.

Indigo leads me toward the golfcart they must have ridden here. I aim for the driver's seat but Virginia groans.

"I know you're heartbroken and I'm supposed to give you whatever you need, but I'm going to puke if the speed demon drives again."

Indigo pushes me out of the way. "I'll drive."

"You're not much better than her."

"I got this." Leia sits in the driver's seat. "I know how to drive with precious cargo aboard."

I sit on the golf cart next to Indigo as we drive away from the garage.

"I could have walked faster than this," I mutter when Leia doesn't increase the speed after joining the main road.

"Feel free to get out and walk," Leia says. "Physical exercise is good for you."

"Is it going to heal my broken heart?" I mutter.

Indigo wraps her arm around my shoulders. "Only time will help."

We reach the house Indigo shares with Cash and pile out of the golf cart.

I pretend to fix my hair. "I don't know, Leia. Any faster and we would have broken the sound barrier."

She bumps my hip. "Be nice. Virginia is feeling queasy."

Indigo's nose wrinkles. "Why are you feeling queasy, Virginia?"

Virginia scans the area. "Not outside. There are spies everywhere."

Once we're settled in the living room, Indigo motions to Virginia. "Are you sick?"

Virginia wrings her hands together. "Not exactly."

Indigo tilts her head and studies her friend. She gasps and her eyes widen. "You're pregnant. Oh my god! You're pregnant!"

She drags Virginia off of the couch and hugs her. Virginia pushes her off. "Queasy remember?"

"Gotcha!" Indigo runs off and returns with an empty trash can seconds later. "I've got you covered."

"How did this happen? And why does Leia know but not me?" Indigo pushes out her bottom lip in a pout. "I'm supposed to be your best friend."

Virginia settles on the sofa with the bucket in her arms. "One, I really hope you know how this happens. And, two, I didn't tell Leia."

"I figured it out when she got queasy while we were driving over to Mercy's garage. I got car sick when I was pregnant with Isla," Leia says.

Indigo settles next to Virginia on the couch. "I guess I forgive you."

"Gee, thanks."

"Congratulations, Virginia. I didn't realize you were trying." I waggle my eyebrows.

"Have you seen Dylan? Of course, I was trying. I want to give him babies and make a family with him."

My stomach sours. I don't know if I'm ready for babies yet, if ever, but I was ready to make a family with Gibson. And Uncle Mercury, of course. I can never forget him.

Virginia glances at me and winces. I guess I'm not hiding my heartbreak very well. "Shoot. I'm sorry, Mercy. Here I am all happy and you're heartbroken."

"It's okay." It's not but at least if we discuss Virginia's happiness we're not discussing my heartbreak.

Indigo blows out a breath. "Good. Because I'm dying to ask about your ring." She points to Virginia's hand.

"Did you just notice the ring?" Leia sighs. "You're not very good at this snooping thing."

"I'm nosy, not a snoop."

"It's good you understand your limitations."

"Dylan and I are engaged and I'm pregnant," Virginia announces. "And now we're done discussing me. We have a heartbroken woman to comfort."

Indigo jumps up. "On it."

"What is she doing?" I ask. "She doesn't have an initiation ceremony for heartbroken women, does she? I'm not drinking a unicorn's tears."

"Don't be silly," Indigo says as she returns with a charcuterie board. "Unicorns don't have tears since they never cry."

She sets the board on the table. My eyes widen at the amount of sugar it contains. There are two bowls filled with chocolate dip as well as berries, candies, cookies, pretzels, and nuts.

"Is sugar supposed to cure a broken heart?" I ask but I don't hesitate to dip a chocolate chip cookie in chocolate and shove it in my mouth.

Indigo's cheeks darken. "Since you don't drink, I thought this was a good idea."

I moan as I chew the cookie. "Not judging you. And I need the recipe for this cookie and dip."

"Great." Indigo rubs her hands together. "Time to get started."

I grab another cookie. If she's going to interrogate me, I deserve some chocolate at least.

"Are there any circumstances under which you would forgive Gibson for what he said and did?"

I narrow my eyes on her. "I get you know we broke up. I wasn't exactly quiet when I returned home last night and Uncle Mercury is a blabbermouth."

"And I saw you leaving Gibson's house," Leia interrupts to say.

"Still, how do you know what Gibson said and did?"

"Trade secret," Indigo claims.

Leia giggles. "Trade secret, my ass. Jett never left. He eavesdropped at the back window."

I groan. "And then he told the whole world my boyfriend thinks I'm a bitch."

"I hate the word bitch," Virginia mutters. She's not the only one. "But Jett did blab to the rest of the band. They're over there now dealing with him."

"Which is why we aren't at my house," Leia says. "No one trusts Gibson to not come after you if he knows where you are."

I snort. "Gibson isn't going to come after me. I told him I loved him and he didn't respond. I think it's safe to say our relationship is dead and buried."

"No, it isn't," Indigo sings.

"Out with it." I'm done playing games. Either she tells me what she knows or I'm getting my hands on her stove. I'm a mechanic. I can cause considerable damage with a gas stove.

"The band gave Gibson an ultimatum," Leia says. "Get sober or they're kicking him out."

I purse my lips. "Ultimatums don't work. Trust me. I know."

"Except." Indigo grins. "When the person given an ultimatum figures the only way to win back the woman he loves is to get sober."

"Gibson doesn't love me."

"Then why did he refuse to go to rehab until after he realized you were done with him?"

I wave away her question. "That doesn't mean he loves me or is getting sober for me."

"Just wait. I'm right about this."

Virginia groans. "Great. She's going to gloat."

Indigo smirks. "I am an excellent gloater."

"Being an excellent gloater is nothing to be proud of."

I tune Indigo and Virginia's bickering out. Is Virginia right? Did Gibson agree to go to rehab because he wants to win me back?

A spark of hope lights in my chest but I douse it with a healthy portion of reality. I've watched my mom go in and out of rehab for years. There's no guarantee of success.

But what if Gibson is different? Hope surfaces once more. I try to douse it again but it's firmly planted in my chest.

Chapter 31

Letter – an ancient method of communication involving pen and paper

GIBSON

I groan as I wake and reach for my phone. My hand meets air. I frown as I open my eyes. My frown deepens when I encounter white walls and utilitarian furniture. This is not the house I'm renting with Jett.

Rehab. For a moment there, I forgot I'm in rehab and miles away from Mercy and my bandmates. I scrub a hand down my face. My usual trimmed beard is out of control after a week of not shaving.

One week down. Who knows how many weeks to go. In the meantime, I'm not allowed to phone or message anyone. No social media. No newsletters. No magazines. Thus, the lack of a phone on my dresser.

I didn't think I was one of those annoying people who is on their phone all the time. I was wrong. I reach for my phone several times an hour. I feel as if I'm missing a limb. I'm cut off from the world and hankering for connection.

I'm desperate to speak to Mercy. To find out how she's doing. How is she handling being a business owner again? And

– most important of all – does she forgive me? Does she still love me? Or does she want nothing to do with me?

Nurse Hannah knocks on the door. "Time for group."

I smile but my usual charm has no effect on Nurse Hannah. She's all business as she motions me toward the room where our group sessions are held.

"Oh, great," Danny says as I enter. "The whiner has arrived."

"I'm not a whiner."

Charles snorts. "Because complaining about how you can't make phone calls for an hour isn't whining."

Danny and Charles are the other members of this group session and they pull no punches. I'll never admit it, but I like both of them. If the circumstances were different, we'd be friends having drinks at a bar.

I scowl at Charles. "I didn't complain for an hour."

Danny chuckles. "And I didn't wet my bed the first night I arrived."

My nose wrinkles. "Gross. Keep your bed wetting stories to yourself."

Charles groans. "Great. Now he thinks you're challenging him."

"I'm not challenging anyone."

Danny wriggles his eyebrows. "Did I tell you about the time I—"

I hold up a hand to stop him. I'll never admit it out loud, but I'm squeamish when it comes to bodily fluids. Bodily fluids should stay where they belong. Inside the body.

Dr. Stu arrives and joins our merry circle. "Good morning."

I open my mouth to ask him what's good about it but slam it shut again when I realize I'd be whining. Damn. I guess I am becoming a whiner.

"Yesterday, we were discussing triggers," Dr. Stu begins. "Charles, you spoke about sports being a trigger for you."

"I started drinking when I got injured playing for the Broncos. It helped me cope with the stress of thinking I was never going to be able to play again," Charles begins.

"Thank you for sharing," Dr. Stu says once Charles has finished his story. "Gibson, you haven't talked much in therapy."

"Except to complain," Danny mutters.

Dr. Stu pretends not to hear Danny. "Do you want to discuss your triggers?"

"No."

Dr. Stu smiles. "Let me rephrase. Tell us about your triggers. It's not a request."

I blow out a breath. The last thing I want to do is discuss my private life with these strangers.

"Anything you say in this group is confidential."

"We're not running to the paps, those vultures," Danny says.

Since he's a movie star and Charles is a former professional athlete who's now a sports commentator, I believe him. They know how the paps can twist a story until it resembles nothing close to the truth just to sell a few more copies. They don't care about causing hurt to those involved. Vultures is too tame a word for them.

"My trigger is my parents. Mostly my dad," I confess.

By the time, the session ends an hour later I feel completely hollowed out. Explaining how my parents are assholes who don't care about me isn't exactly fun.

Dr. Stu stands. "Tomorrow we'll discuss coping strategies."

Danny and Charles hurry out of the room but Dr. Stu motions for me to stay behind.

"Thanks for sharing today."

I grunt. It's not as if I had a choice.

"Nurse Hannah told me you've complained about not being able to make any phone calls. As I explained to you before, you'll only be allowed access to your phone after the initial fourteen days."

"That's another week away." Another week without contact with Mercy. Will she have forgotten about me by then?

"True, but there are other methods of communicating with people."

I frown. "I can't message her without a phone."

He chuckles. "How about a letter?"

"A letter?"

"I instructed Nurse Hannah to place some paper and envelopes in your room," he says before someone hollers his name. He rushes off as I contemplate his words.

A letter? What would I say to Mercy in a letter? I usually fly by the seat of my pants. Writing a letter takes planning and consideration. Two things I'm not exactly known for.

I return to my room to find a pile of paper on my desk. I pick up a pen and twirl it around as I contemplate what to write.

Dear Mercy,

I tap the pen against the desk. Great start. I'm not a song-writer. Cash is the songwriter of the band. I don't have fancy words of love for Mercy. I can't write her a ballad that becomes a hit song.

But I do need her to forgive me. To give me another chance. Because I love her.

I can't write her a letter claiming I love her now though. She won't believe me. And I wouldn't blame her either. Besides, she deserves to hear those words in person.

What I can do is apologize. And explain.

I start again.

Dear Mercy,

I'm not allowed to speak to you on the phone yet. Apparently, I whined about the no phone situation a bit much since I returned to my room to find a pen and paper on my desk.

I'm not the songwriter of the band, but I'll try to put my thoughts into writing. I hope you read this and don't burn it the second it arrives. I wouldn't blame you, though. I was a complete and utter asshole to you.

I'm sorry for the way I treated you. If I'm completely honest –something these doctors in rehab say I should be – I don't remember the night very well.

The guys filled me in. Who knows how they know every single thing that happened – the gossip gals probably have our house bugged – but they did.

~~I can't believe I called you a bitch.~~

I scratch those words out. It doesn't matter what I believe. And saying I can't believe it kind of nullifies the apology. It happened. I need to own up to my behavior.

I'm sorry I called you a bitch. I know the word is a trigger for you. I'm learning all about triggers here.

Speaking of triggers…

My dad rang me that day. He wanted me to buy him a new car because the Mercedes I bought them is too old now.

I'm not trying to excuse my behavior – there is no excuse for it – but maybe an explanation will help you understand why I did what I did.

I've always drank a bit too much. It's easy to get carried away when you're on tour and alcohol is shoved into your hands at every turn. Fame is intoxicating – pun intended – when it first happens and before you realize it's all a smoke screen.

But when my parents sued me I started drinking more to numb the pain. Their lawsuit felt like a rejection of my love for them. Why else would they demand money from me? And insist they were the only reason I became famous?

If they loved me, they wouldn't have sued me is what I thought. There must have been something wrong with me to prevent them from loving me.

And so I drank.

Dr. Stu says I need to learn coping mechanisms to stop myself from reaching for a beer whenever I'm triggered. I'm not there yet but I'm not leaving this place until I am. I'm pretty sure the good 'ol doc is hatching a plan, which involves me phoning my parents before I'm allowed to leave. Something to look forward to.

I'm sorry again for the things I said. The way I acted. I can't apologize enough for how I acted.

Or for breaking your trust. I promised not to drink as long as we were dating and I broke my promise. ~~Can you ever forgive me?~~

I cross out the last question. I want Mercy to forgive me and give me a second chance more than anything in the world. But it's too early to ask for her forgiveness. I need to show her she can trust me first.

I miss you, sassy girl. I miss the twinkle in your eye before you sass at me. I miss watching you try to bring Mercury into line. I miss your insistence on listening to country music. I miss how fast you drive. Your smile when you switch on the car engine. I miss how you refuse to care I'm a rockstar. Have you googled me yet?

I'll write again soon.

Yours always,

Guitar man

I fold the paper and stick it into the envelope.

Step one in my plan to get my girl back is underway. Go to rehab and get sober.

Step two is to get Mercy to forgive me. This letter is the start.

Step three is for Mercy to give me another chance. No sense worrying about a second chance until she's forgiven me.

But I am not letting Mercy go without a fight. She owns my heart and soul.

Please forgive me, Mercy. I don't want to live without you. I can't.

Chapter 32

Nosy – an understatement with regard to the inhabitants of Winter Falls

Mercy

"The mail's here," Uncle Mercury shouts. "You better run out there and check if your young man wrote you today."

I glare at him. "You're not supposed to know about the letters from Gibson."

He chuckles. "You swoon whenever you receive one. It's not hard to figure out."

"I don't swoon," I grumble and rush outside to the mailbox.

Rain, the mayor who also happens to be the mailperson, is waiting on me. "There's another one."

"You're not supposed to snoop in my mail."

She snorts. "All I did was read the return address."

Now, it makes sense how Uncle Mercury knows about the letters. Rain has been tattling to everyone in town. Sometimes I wonder why I chose to stay in this small town.

I raise my eyebrows. "And tell everyone in town about the letters?"

She shrugs. "We're concerned about you is all."

Concerned my ass. They're taking bets on when Gibson will return and whether I'll forgive him. Apparently, the residents in this town will bet on anything.

Rain pats my hand. "I know it feels as if everyone in town is a busybody but I promise you everyone is concerned. It's no small thing to get sober."

I blow out a breath. "No, it isn't."

"We're on your side, Mercy," she says before hopping on her bike and peddling away.

My eyes itch as I watch her. No one's ever been on my side before and now a whole town is? It's enough to make a girl cry. I blink my eyes and force the tears away. Uncle Mercury won't know what to do with himself if he sees me crying.

"You ready?" Indigo shouts as she stops next to me in a golfcart. Virginia, Leia, and Leia's daughter, Isla, are with her.

I glance down at the letter. I want to read it before we go to today's festival.

"Hurry up, Mercy," Isla shouts. "Mom is being mean and says I can only stay out for a few hours."

Leia sighs. "Your bedtime doesn't disappear because there's a festival in town."

"Dad says it does."

"Your father is a pushover," Leia mumbles.

I shove the letter in my back pocket. I'll read it when I'm alone. Now is the moment to spend time with my friends. The friends who have gotten me through the past month while Gibson's been away.

I sit on the back of the golfcart. "I'm ready."

"You can read Gibson's letter while I drive us," Indigo suggests.

"No," Virginia insists. "She's not going to read the letter out loud so you can get inside information to place your bet."

I groan. "Cash will probably know when Gibson will return before me. Ask him and place your bet."

Leia grins. "She's not interested in betting on when Gibson will return. She wants to know if you're going to forgive him."

"Do you love Uncle Gibson, Mercy?" Isla asks.

Good question. I fell in love with the Gibson he showed me. The fun guy who made me laugh but was also there for me when Uncle Mercury got sick. The man who showed me what real passion is in the bedroom.

But do I love Gibson now? The man who struggles with demons and uses booze to numb his pain?

I shouldn't. I should know better than to love a man who deals with addiction every day.

But I'm not giving up on him because he's addicted. It's not who I am. I will stand by Gibson and lift him up when he stumbles. Be his strength when he runs out. Love him even when I want to kick his teeth out.

"You love him," Isla announces.

"How do you know?"

She rolls her eyes. "You have the same mushy look on your face when you think of him as Mom does when she looks at Dad."

I bump her shoulder. "How did you get this smart?"

"Dad says I get it from him but he's lying since he's not my bio dad."

"You're smart."

She beams at me. "I'm the smartest of my class."

"Good for you."

"We know Mercy loves Gibson. She's been walking around all mopey for a month without him," Indigo says and I stick my tongue out at her. "The question is – will she forgive him?"

Of course, I forgive him. Maybe I'm a walking doormat or an idiot or can't stop making the wrong decisions about men, but I don't care. A man who's willing to go to rehab – and stay – and sends me letters of apology every day deserves to be forgiven and given a second chance.

But if he ever calls me bitch again I'm hitting him over the head with a wrench and burying him in the forest where no one will find him.

"Forgive him for what?" Isla asks.

I glare at Indigo. I'm not explaining what happened to a twelve-year-old. "Thanks."

"Oops! Sorry." She doesn't appear sorry at all.

"I hope your children are exactly like you."

Virginia smiles as she rubs her belly. "I hope my baby takes after Dylan."

"Virginia already said I can babysit her baby," Isla says. "I'm going to be the best babysitter."

I ruffle her hair. "I bet you will."

We arrive downtown and Indigo parks the golfcart.

"What's today's festival all about anyway?" I ask as we walk to Main Street.

I'm surprised when I scan the area and it's not completely packed with people. Usually the Winter Falls' festivals attract tons of tourists. It's how most of the businesses in town manage to survive.

Indigo starts to answer but doesn't get a chance before Sage calls out.

"Did you get a letter today?" she ask as she marches toward us with her gossip gal entourage – Feather, Petal, Cayenne, and Clove – trailing her.

"Did you get a letter today?" Sage repeats her question once she reaches us.

"Good afternoon, Sage. It's lovely to see you, too. I'm well. Thanks for asking."

Petal giggles. "I love a sassy heroine."

I roll my eyes. "I'm not a heroine in one of your sexy romance books."

"How would you know?" Feather asks. "You never come to sexy book club."

Clove purses her lips at me. "And you promised you would."

I wag a finger at her. "I never promised. If I had promised, I would have been there."

Good thing I didn't promise because I always keep my promises. But I haven't had time to attend book club. I've been working on building my business, *Wheely Great.* There have been loan agreements to review, purchase agreements to read, and years of administration Basil ignored to try and organize.

Plus, the actual business of restoring classic cars. I was worried about finding customers but it turns out Basil had a long waiting list. I don't have to bother with customer recruitment for years.

Cayenne studies me. "I think she's going to forgive him."

I sigh. Of course, the gossip gals surrounded me because they want to butt into my life.

Feather smiles. "Of course, she's forgiving him. He's been sending her love letters every day for a month. Any woman would forgive him."

"The question I want to know the answer to is," Sage leans in close. "Will she give him a second chance and when?"

I hold up my hands. "Why is everyone all up in my business today?"

Cayenne snorts. "This is our first chance to bother you. You usually have your head stuck under the hood of a car."

I frown. "I thought you gossip gals were all for equality between men and women. There's nothing wrong with having my head stuck in an engine."

"There is when you're using work as an excuse to avoid us," Sage says.

"I wish I could use work as an excuse to avoid them," Virginia mumbles next to me. "But the library is a public place."

Cash, Dylan, Fender, and Jett stroll over to us. My stomach falls and sadness fills me. It's always difficult seeing the band without Gibson with them.

I hope he comes home soon. He hasn't mentioned when he'll be released, so I'm assuming it'll be another few weeks.

I miss him but I want him to have the best chance of staying sober, which means being away from me. Too bad visits aren't allowed.

"Jett!" Isla shouts and runs to him. He picks her up and whirls her around.

"How are you doing, squirt?"

Fender glares at him. "She's my daughter."

Jett rolls his eyes. "Don't be a daughter hog." He sets Isla on the ground. "*Bake Me Happy* has chocolate chip cookies on sale. You want one?"

"You can't bribe my daughter with cookies," Fender grumbles.

"Can I go, Dad? Can I?" Isla bats her eyelashes at him.

"One cookie and you'll come back here," Leia says.

Isla and Jett skip off. I frown after them. Jett's been avoiding me since Gibson went into rehab. He's never warmed to me but he's Gibson's best friend. I don't want Gibson to have to choose between us.

Cash crosses his arms over his chest and glares at the gossip gals. I step back. I don't want to be involved in this confrontation.

"You promised you'd stay out of it."

"We are," Sage claims.

"Can't we watch?" Feather asks.

"Watch what?" I ask. I guess I want to be involved after all.

"Nothing," Cash grunts.

"You're having a confrontation over nothing?"

"My sassy girl hasn't changed one bit."

Hold on. There's only one person who calls me sassy girl. I whirl around and gasp when Gibson waves at me.

"Gibson!" I scream and run to him. He catches me in his arms. I want to enjoy the feel of his arms around me, his warmth surrounding me, but I have questions. I push away from him.

"You're out! Why didn't you tell me? When did you get back? Why didn't you ask me to pick you up? I would have."

Chapter 33

Sneak attack – when the visitor you don't want to see shows up unexpectedly

GIBSON

I hold out my hand to Mercy and pray she'll take it. "Can we talk somewhere private?"

"Boo!" Sage yells behind me.

"We wouldn't have arranged this festival for you if we knew you were going to hide from us," Clove claims.

Mercy's brow wrinkles. "Arrange this festival for you? What are they talking about?"

I wiggle my hand. "Come with me and I'll explain."

She slaps her hand in mine. "This better be one awesome explanation."

I lead her down the street until we reach *Bake Me Happy*. I made arrangements with Bryan to get some privacy here. I haven't lived in Winter Falls long but I knew I'd need somewhere private to talk because otherwise the entire town is going to listen in on our conversation.

We enter and I frown when I notice Jett and Isla are here. Isla sees me and breaks away from Jett to run for me.

"You're home!"

She flies at me and I catch her and whirl her around. "I'm home."

"Good. Mercy was sad when you were gone."

Mercy groans behind me and I cough to hide my smile.

I didn't know what kind of reception I'd face with Mercy. Despite my daily letters to me, she never wrote back. And then I got the crazy idea to keep writing letters and not phone her. To wait to speak to her until I was released.

Jett holds out his hand to Isla. "Let's go and leave these two alone."

Isla picks up a cookie the size of her face before grasping Jett's hand.

"Bye," Mercy calls as they leave. Isla waves but Jett doesn't respond.

"He doesn't like me," Mercy says once the door is closed behind them.

"He likes you. But he's mad at me."

"Mad at you? How dare he? You're working your ass off to get sober and he's mad? Is he bummed to lose a drinking partner?" She starts for the door. "I'll talk to him."

I shackle her wrist to stop her. "He's not mad I got sober. He's not worried about losing a drinking partner. He's mad I broke our pact not to fall in love."

She freezes. "What did you say?"

I pull her near and place my hands on her hips. "I love you, Mercy Keller."

Her mouth drops open. "You love me?"

I kiss her nose. "I love you, my sassy girl."

Her eyes narrow. "Is this some big discovery you made in rehab?"

"Nope. I knew I loved you before I left for rehab. It's the main reason I agreed to go."

"You didn't agree to rehab because the band was kicking you out if you didn't get sober?"

I sigh. "Heard about that, did you?"

"It's Winter Falls."

Bryan chuckles as he enters the bakery from the kitchen. "Never mind me." He holds up two mugs. "I just wanted to get you two coffees before I leave you alone."

I usher Mercy to a table away from the window.

"I put on the closed sign and the front door is locked," Bryan announces as he places our drinks on the table.

Mercy stares at him. "You're going to leave us alone? You're not going to stand across the room and pretend not to listen?" She narrows her eyes at him. "Did you plant bugs in here?"

"I did not plant bugs." Bryan sounds indignant. I can't resist bursting his righteous bubble.

"I paid him to give us the bakery for an hour."

He harrumphs. "You had to tell her?" He whirls around and flounces off. "Rockstars. I'll never understand them."

"You're just mad because you hit on Adam and he turned you town," I holler after him.

His response is to slam the back door. Such a drama queen.

"Who's Adam?" Mercy asks.

I hate the doubt creeping into her voice. She doesn't trust me anymore. Not after I broke my promise to her. I don't blame her. I have to be patient while I earn her trust back.

"Remember I told you about the band I helped out while they were recording here?" She nods. "Adam is the bass player."

"Ah."

I sip on my coffee while I figure out how to begin. "Did you get my letters?"

"I did."

"Did you read them or did you burn them behind Uncle Mercury's house while he cheered you on?"

She fiddles with the edge of the table but I notice her cheeks darken. "I read them."

"Thank you."

"Why are you thanking me?"

I reach across the table and place my hand over hers. "Because you read my letters despite how pissed you must have been at me."

"I wasn't pissed," she mumbles.

"You weren't?" My sassy girl has a temper.

She blows out a breath. "I was heartbroken."

My heart hammers in my chest and I squeeze her hand. "I'm sorry. I'm such an idiot. You told me you loved me and I called you a bitch."

She flinches at the word bitch.

"I promise never to call you a bitch again." I inhale a deep breath and continue. "And I promise to never drink again."

She scowls. "No."

"No? You don't want me to be sober? I'm confused."

"Of course, I want you to stay sober. By the way, I'm proud of you for going to rehab and sticking with it." She squeezes my hand. "Not everyone with a problem does."

I tuck a strand of her hair behind her ear. "I'm sorry about your mom."

She leans into my hand for comfort and a spark of hope fills me. She's not pushing me away. She's listening to me. Maybe she will give me a second chance.

"Why don't you want me to promise to stay sober?"

She clears her throat. "I want you to promise to try your best to stay sober. I don't want you to cave under the pressure of promising me to stay sober."

I don't hesitate. "I promise I will do my best to stay sober. I've found a local support group in White Bridge and one of their members already agreed to be my sponsor."

She smiles and steals my breath away. I didn't think I was ever going to see her smile again. At least not directed at me.

"I love you, sassy girl. Will you give me another chance to earn your trust?"

"I—"

"Mercy Keller," a woman screams and pounds on the window. "I know you're in there! I can see you! You can't ignore me any longer!"

Mercy buries her face in her hands and groans.

"Who is it?" I ask but considering the woman is weaving as she tries to stay upright I think I can guess.

"My mom," she says as she starts to stand.

I move to stop her. "No. You don't deal with her anymore. I do."

"You can't fight my battles for me."

"Watch me."

I march to the front door. Mercy follows me but I don't try to stop her again. My sassy girl doesn't enjoy being bossed around unless we're in the bedroom.

"Who are you?" Mercy's mom asks when I fling the door open.

Mercy grunts behind me. "Mom, this is Gibson. Gibson, this is my mom, Estelle."

I stand in front of Mercy to block her mother from seeing her. "You deal with me."

"I don't know you. Who the hell are you?"

"I'm the man standing in front of the woman I love making sure her mother doesn't hurt her anymore."

Mercy digs her fingers into my belt buckle. I pat her arm. I've got this.

"I need to speak to my daughter."

I cross my arms and glare at the woman. "All communication goes through me."

"Don't want you." She waves me away and loses her balance. She stumbles before managing to right herself.

"What do you want to speak with Mercy about?"

"I bet I know," Sage says as she and the rest of the gossip gals join us.

Estelle scans the area and scowls when she realizes she's surrounded by the entire town. Mercy's friends and my bandmates move to stand behind us.

Their silent support means the world to me. I worried I'd lost my family when they threatened to kick me out of *Cash & the Sinners.*

But Dylan confessed on the ride into town from rehab today how their threat was an empty one. They would have never forced me out of the band. Let alone abandoned me.

Feather snorts. "We all know."

Petal nods. "She wants Mercury's money."

"It's my money," Estelle shrieks.

"It's not your money," Sage says. "It's Mercury's money. He can do with it what he wants."

Estelle snarls at Mercy. "And I bet he bought your little innocent act."

I step forward. "Don't you dare speak to her that way. You don't deserve to breathe the same air as her. Let along be a witch to her."

"She's my daughter. I'll say whatever I want to her."

I growl. "You're done. You can walk away from Winter Falls of your own accord or I will walk you out of here."

Sage hustles to my side. "We got this."

The gossip gals surround Estelle and herd her away from us.

"I'll make sure she doesn't come back and the gossip gals stay in control," Peace says as he follows them.

"Show's over, folks," I announce in a loud voice once Estelle is gone.

"But what about the community dinner we arranged?" Indigo asks.

"The community dinner?" Mercy asks.

Indigo points to me. "Your guitar man wanted to have a celebration with the entire town upon his return."

"We'll be there in a minute," I say.

Cash clutches Indigo's hand. "Come on. Let's go."

"But I want to watch Gibson grovel," she whines but Cash drags her away.

The rest of the group dispenses. Once they're gone, I turn to Mercy. "I hope I wasn't out of line with your mom."

"Second chance granted!" She yells and flings herself at me.

I meld my lips to hers. I moan when she immediately opens to me. I never thought I'd experience her spicy taste again. I thought I'd lost her forever. But I didn't. I will spend my life exploring this woman's mouth and body. My cock twitches in response.

I slow the kiss until I can break away. "Love you, sassy girl."

She smiles at me. "I love you, too, Gibson."

"I promise I won't break your heart again."

"Good because I have the plot all picked out where I want to bury you if you do."

I chuckle. This woman will keep me on my toes for the rest of my life. I can't wait.

"What the hell?" Jett shouts. "What are you doing here?"

I glance over to discover Jett glaring down at Aurora.

"Is this the mysterious Aurora?" Mercy whispers.

I nod.

She steps away and grasps my hand. "Come on. Let's go be nosy."

I follow her. I'll always follow her. Wherever she goes, I go from now on.

Chapter 34

Aurora – a woman who's about to blow a rockstar's life apart

AURORA

I sigh as I cross the border into Winter Falls. Despite being the personal assistant of *Cash & the Sinners*, I haven't visited the town yet. I prefer to keep away from certain members of the band.

I glance down at my stomach. I guess that ship has sailed now.

I notice the sign for *The Inn on Main*, the only place to stay in town, and turn left into the parking lot. I'm surprised how few cars there are considering the owner said the only room available was a suite.

Whatever. It doesn't matter. My boss – Mike the band manager – is paying for the room anyway. I convinced him I need to be in Winter Falls since the band has settled here.

I walk to the entrance of the bed and breakfast. It's cute. What I've seen of the town thus far is cute. I can understand why the band wanted to settle here.

Except Jett. He's not going to settle anywhere as boring as a small town. His words. Not mine.

I enter through the front door and scan the area. It's as adorable as the outside. The entry is wide with a small reception desk off to the side. To the other side is an entry into a cozy looking sitting room. In front of me is a small seating area with cookies and coffee.

I eye the cookies and my stomach rumbles in response.

"Help yourself," the woman at the reception desk says. "I'll be with you in a minute."

In that case … I study the cookies. There is a variety. Chocolate chip, oatmeal raisin, and something with nuts. I pick up an oatmeal raisin. Oatmeal is healthy, isn't it?

I bite into the cookie and moan. Holy cow this is yummy.

The receptionist giggles. "I have the same reaction whenever I eat a cookie from *Bake Me Happy*."

"This cookie can bake me happy anytime."

"I'm Ellery, the owner of *The Inn on Main*, and you must be Aurora."

She holds out her hand and I wipe the cookie crumbs on my shirt before shaking hers.

"Sorry, I've been driving for days."

"You're fine." She glances around me. "Where's your luggage?"

"In the car, I didn't feel up to dragging it inside."

"Let me show you to your room and then I'll have someone deal with your luggage."

Her words are music to my ears. I've been schlepping my suitcases in and out of motels for three days. I'm ready to spend more than eight hours in one place.

We climb two sets of stairs before we reach the attic.

Ellery opens the door to the only room on this floor. "The executive suite. It's my favorite room. The bathroom is through there. You have a bathtub and a separate shower. You'll find extra bedding in the closet but with the fireplace you should be warm enough."

Fireplace? I somehow missed the large fireplace across from the bed. There's a comfy looking chair in front of it. This place is nearly as large as my apartment in San Diego. It's definitely nicer.

"You said you'd be working while here?"

I nod.

"There's free Wi-Fi and if you need anything printed, let me know. There's also a kitchenette but breakfast is included in your nightly rate."

The kitchenette isn't much. A two-burner stove next to a sink with a cupboard above it. It'll do for now.

"You can also eat at the diner or the brewery. They're both open for lunch and dinner."

I won't be eating at the brewery, but a local small town diner sounds good. "Thank you."

"I'll leave you to settle in. I'll have your luggage sent up."

I cross to the bay window with its view over the town. Main Street stretches out in front of me. There aren't any cars on the road but I didn't expect any. Not after the amount of times Jett complained about the 'crazy environmental rules' in Winter Falls.

Stores line the street. Judging by the names I can read –
Naked Falls Brewing and *Electric Vibes* to name a few – the town
is as quirky as I expected.

I rub a hand over my stomach. I'd love to settle down in a
small town. I have no desire to remain in San Diego where I
can barely afford my rent and don't know my neighbors.

A large group of people are gathering near several long tables
set up around the square. I wonder what's happening.

"Knock! Knock!" Ellery hollers before entering and placing
my suitcases next to the door.

"Do you know what's going on?" I point outside to the town
square.

"It's a town celebration."

"To celebrate what?"

She frowns. "You're not a reporter, are you?"

I bark out a laugh. "Nope. And I hate paps more than you
do." I clear my throat. "I'm actually the personal assistant for
Cash & the Sinners. It's why I'm here."

I'm lying. I can easily do my work from a distance. I don't
need to be in town to cater to every whim the band has.

Ellery studies me. "How do I know you're not lying and
you're actually one of the paps? We kick all of the paps out of
town. No hotel refunds."

I dig out my phone and scan my pics until I find one with
me and the band. "This good enough?"

"Wow." She says as she studies the picture. "They look
young here."

"It was during their first tour." She hands my phone back to me and I scroll through the pictures to find a more recent one. "This was a few months ago."

"You look hot with a guitar."

"Too bad I can't actually play one. I didn't get a job at a managing firm as a gateway to fame. Mike hired me because I don't take crap from anyone." Including Jett, the supreme asshole of the universe.

Ellery smiles at me. "Good for you." She motions to the window. "The celebration is for Gibson. He got out of rehab today."

"Today?" I consult my agenda. "He's not supposed to get out for another five days. Shit. I need to speak with him."

I grab my coat from the bed where I threw it. "This job never ends."

"Tell me about it," Ellery mutters.

I say my good-byes and hurry out of the inn and down Main Street to where the party is happening. I roll my eyes. I don't think a party is a good way to celebrate being sober but what do I know?

I scan the area for Gibson but my gaze gets stuck on Jett. He's not alone.

My mouth gapes open at the vision in front of me. Jett is playing with a girl. I'd guess she's around thirteen. As I watch, the girl touches him and yells *You're it.* Jett bounds away but stops after a few steps to make sure she can keep up.

I rub my eyes. I must be seeing things. The Jett I know absolutely does not want anything to do with children. It's why I've kept things secret from him.

I'll deal with him later. Gibson is my current priority. I spot him making out with a woman on the sidewalk. She must be Mercy.

I've been looking forward to meeting her. Too bad our first meeting will involve me yelling at her boyfriend for busting out of rehab early.

I march toward them.

"What the hell?" Jett's shout has me stopping in my tracks. "What are you doing here? Are you stalking me?"

"Wow. How big is your ego? I'm not stalking you. I'm the PA for the band or did the bump on your head give you amnesia."

The rest of the band and their partners gather around us. Awesome. An audience.

"You won't be the PA any longer if I have anything to do with it," Jett grumbles.

I throw my arms in the air. "Not this again. How many times are you going to try and get me fired?"

He doesn't respond. Probably because he's too busy staring at my bump.

"Are you pregnant?"

I place a protective hand over my stomach.

"You are. It better not be fucking mine," he says and stalks off.

My breath catches and tears well in my eyes. I knew he wouldn't handle my being pregnant with his baby well, but this is worse than anything I could have imagined.

I whirl around and rush away. I can't deal with the sympathy from the rest of the band now.

Chapter 35

Happy ever after – when everyone gets what they want even Old Man Mercury

Mercy

"Hello! Is anyone home?" I holler as I enter Uncle Mercury's house.

Uncle Mercury is usually sitting in his ratty armchair when I arrive home. But he's nowhere to be seen. Neither is whoever is supposed to be watching him today.

I dig my phone out. I have a schedule of which gossip gal is watching Mercury when in here somewhere.

"We're out back," Gibson shouts.

What is he doing here? Granted Gibson lives here now with me and Mercury, but he wasn't supposed to be home today. He had 'band stuff' to do. Whatever that means.

I open the back door to find Gibson waiting for me.

I push up on my toes to kiss him. "Hi, guitar man."

"Hey, sassy girl," he whispers against my lips.

"Are you going to kiss all day?" Uncle Mercury asks and we pull apart.

"Hi, Uncle Mercury. How was your day? Speaking of days, what are you doing home?" I ask Gibson.

He smiles. "We have a surprise for you."

"The two of you have a surprise for me?" I ask and he nods. "Oh boy. I hope it isn't how you 'accidentally' caused a hole in the side of the house again."

Gibson rolls his eyes. "It was an accident and it wasn't a hole. Just a little dent in the wall."

It was a hole. I really didn't think I needed to make a rule about playing baseball in the house.

"Come on," Uncle Mercury orders. "I ain't got all day."

"Oh yeah? What do you need to do, Mercury? Got a hot date later? Who is it? Cayenne or Feather?"

He scowls at me. "I'm not dating those women."

I waggle my eyebrows. "They beg to differ."

"Follow me," he orders.

I hurry to him when he reaches the stairs off the back patio. He shoos me away.

"I can walk stairs. I'm not an invalid."

Uncle Mercury will be on his death bed and claiming he's not an invalid. I ignore him and grasp his elbow to steady him as he maneuvers the three steps down to the yard.

He starts off across the lawn and that's when I see it.

"There's a tiny house in the back yard!" I exclaim.

Gibson wraps an arm around my shoulders. "What do you think?"

"It's cute. Is it for us?" I rub my hands together. "This is exciting. I can't wait to look inside."

"Don't you go stealing my home, Mercy," Mercury grumbles.

"Your home? You have a home." I indicate the house behind us.

He points to the tiny house with his cane. "This is mine."

"Everyone needs to slow down. How did this tiny house get here? Why is Uncle Mercury moving out of his home?"

"The tiny house was delivered today. It's not ready to use yet. The builders estimate it'll be finished and ready for use in two to three weeks," Gibson explains.

"But I thought you were prepping to build a studio in the back yard." The concrete slabs he had poured are supposed to be for his studio.

"I don't need a studio."

"You tricked me?"

He grins. "I tricked you."

"But why is Uncle Mercury saying the tiny house is his home? He already has a home."

"The house is yours," Mercury says.

I try to find some patience. We've been arguing over who owns the house for months. I say it's his. He doesn't agree.

"As long as you're alive the house is yours," I start.

He smirks. "Not any longer."

I narrow my eyes on him. "What did you do?"

He waves his cane at Gibson. "Not me. Your boyfriend."

I switch my glare to Gibson. "What did you do?"

He grasps my hand and pulls me forward. "Why don't we check out Mercury's new house first?"

Sneaky bastard. He knows I hate fighting in front of my uncle since Mercury doesn't hesitate to give his opinion. And he tends to agree with Gibson more often than not. The two men are always ganging up on me.

"Fine," I mutter and march to the tiny house. I open the door and help Mercury inside before scanning the area.

"This is the living room slash kitchen dining area," Gibson explains. "To the left is the bathroom. On the opposite side is the bedroom. There's even a small washing area."

I snort. "Because Uncle Mercury does so much laundry."

"Why would I do laundry when I've got an able-bodied niece to do it for me?" Mercury asks.

My uncle is perfectly cable of doing everything by himself unless it involves washing clothes, cleaning dishes, or cooking meals. Anytime one of those activities comes up, he's suddenly unable to stand and his bones ache.

"What do you think?" Gibson asks.

"It's adorable. It's perfect for us."

He tweaks my nose. "Nice try. We're living in the big house, sassy girl."

"My show is on," Uncle Mercury announces. "I'll meet you back at the house."

I hurry to help him but he shoos me away. "I can walk."

I help him out of the door anyway and then watch as he maneuvers the path to the house. Only once he's climbed the three stairs and entered the house do I turn around to confront Gibson.

I plant my fists on my hips. "What the hell is going on?"

He steps toward me but I hold up my hand. "Stop. You are not using your charm on me today, guitar man."

He winks. "But you admit I'm charming."

"I admit I'm going to use the plot of land I picked out to bury you in if you don't explain yourself soon."

"Uncle Mercury wants you to have his house."

"Tell me something I don't know," I mumble.

"But you don't want his house because you don't want him to think you're taking care of him for money."

I cross my arms over my chest. "I'm not taking care of him for some reward."

"I know, sassy girl. You hide a soft heart underneath your sass."

"What's your point?" I ask since I'm not discussing having a soft heart.

"I want you to have Mercury's house, he wants you to have his house, and I know you want the house."

"You know everything, do you?"

"I know this is the first place you've ever felt you had a home." He steps closer. "It's the same for me. This is the first home I've had in over a decade. I don't want to lose it."

"What did you do?"

"I solved the problem. I bought the house from Mercury. And Mercury bought this tiny house."

"Mercury sold you his house?"

"Technically, he sold it to you since it'll be in your name."

"I can't afford a mortgage. I'm barely handling the payments for the garage as it is."

Gibson palms my neck and squeezes. "Mercury doesn't want you to repay the money he gave you for the garage."

"I don't accept charity."

"It's not charity. Mercury wants you to have the money." He kisses my forehead. "He doesn't have any other relatives. And he feels bad for never contacting your mother. He feels guilty he didn't help you when you were growing up."

"It wasn't his responsibility."

"He feels otherwise."

My eyes itch and I glance away. Uncle Mercury hasn't come out and said it but I know he wishes he'd been there for me when I was a child. It means the world to me to know he wishes he could have shared the burden with me.

"You want to thank him for all he's done for you? This is the way."

My brow furrows. "By accepting his money?"

"Yes."

I blow out a breath. "Fine."

"You'll accept the arrangement?"

He doesn't wait for me to respond before melding his lips to mine. A spark ignites in my belly when we touch. It always does. I hope it always will.

"I love you, sassy girl."

"And I love you, guitar man."

There's a knock on the door. "Uncle Mercury says no having sex in his house," Indigo shouts through the door.

I groan and bury my face in Gibson's shoulder. "What is she doing here?"

"I'm your bestie! Of course, I'm here."

Gibson sighs. "Leia saw the tiny house being delivered and phoned to find out what's happened. And then the gossip gals showed up. Things kind of snowballed from there."

I chuckle. "Living in Winter Falls will never be boring."

Gibson pinches my chin and lifts my head up. "Life with you will never be boring. I love you."

"I'll never get tired of hearing those words."

"Good since I plan to tell you I love you on a daily basis."

About the author

D.E. Haggerty is an American who has spent the majority of her adult life abroad. She has lived in Istanbul, various places throughout Germany, and currently finds herself in The Hague. She has been a military policewoman, a lawyer, a B&B owner/operator and now a writer.

Printed in Great Britain
by Amazon

44751901R00169